Lucifer's Angel

By
R.W.K. Clark

Published in the United States by Clarkltd.
Po Box 45313 Rio Rancho, NM 87174
info@clarkltd.com

Edition 1

United States Copyright Office
TX8-284-097 June 2016

Library of Congress Control Number: 2017907155

International Standard Book Numbers
ISBN-13: 978-0692733288 (Paperback)
ISBN-13: 978-1948312219 (Paperback)
ISBN-13: 978-1948312226 (Hardback)
ASIN: B01GN0IPTS (Kindle)

/200801

PRAISES FOR LUCIFER'S ANGEL

"Excellent story with a mind-bending twist. I thought about the ending for a couple of days after reading it."
— *Ink Spill on amazon*

"One book that did get my goosebumps popping."
— *Charliesullivan on barnesandnoble*

"Took me by the hair and flung me off in a direction I could have never expected or saw coming. Incredible!"
— *Cadenroberts on barnesandnoble*

"Surprised me with an ending that is nothing short of astonishing."
— *Donnellc on barnesandnoble*

"Enough twists and turns to keep you heart beating fast. The ending is a shocker."
— *Freespirit on amazon*

"An emotional rollercoaster ride, and at many junctures, I couldn't figure out which direction Sarah would go."
— *LJ on amazon*

"Completely spun me around from any expectations I had. This is an incredible book!"
— *Clarksbrooklyn on barnesandnoble*

"A horror delight, and nothing in the book was really as it seemed."

— *Samanthaenq on barnesandnoble*

"The ending had such a good twist, I had no idea, wow what a mind blow."

— *Yania on amazon*

"Definitely a great book for anyone who loves surprises!"

— *Milesgran on barnesandnoble*

"A must-read for any young person who is considering jumping before they learn about the waters below."

— *Brycenscott on barnesandnoble*

"Even though this book is out of my Christian genre I highly recommend you read this book you won't regret it."

— *Rosellobo on barnesandnoble*

"A paranormal thriller you can't put down. I highly recommend it."

— *Rhodorah on barnesandnoble*

"You must pick up this book! The ending will throw you for a loop!"

— *Christoreyes on barnesandnoble*

CONTENTS

ACKNOWLEDGMENTS

I dedicate this novel to my wonderful readers and for all the amazing people I've met and those I haven't. To my family and loved ones, all your support will not be forgotten.

This book was made possible by reviews from readers like you.

Thank you

R.W.K. Clark

CHAPTER 1

"Everyone who plans on participating in the Christmas play needs to be prepared for an audition next Wednesday night, after evening services." Mrs. Bailey was saying as she addressed the teenager's Sunday school class, "Myself and Mrs. Holt, the pianist, will be supervising the auditions and assigning roles, with exception to the younger classes, who will participate as choir members."

Sarah Hathaway loved this time of year. Not only was it Christmas, but she got to participate in the church's drama program with three rehearsals a week. This was so exciting to Sarah because this meant spending time alone with her grandmother Emma Holt, the pianist. Her grandmother was her favorite person in the world. Typically, she only got to spend time with her at services and every other weekend, but during the holiday season, she and her grandmother were nearly inseparable.

"So," Miriam Bailey continued, "know which part you are trying out for ahead of time and learn a scene featuring the character you wish to portray." She lifted a stack of scripts off the desk at the front of the room to pass out. "Sarah, will you please help me pass these out?"

Sarah jumped to her feet without hesitation. "Yes, ma'am."

"As you all know, not everyone in this room will get a part with lines. Some of you will be assigned as 'extras,' like in the movies." Mrs. Bailey and Sarah began to pass out the scripts as she spoke. "Please do not write in these. Be a good steward of church property, please. I want these back in the same condition they are in right now."

When the scripts were in the students' hands, Mrs. Bailey gave a broad smile to the entire class. "This is a wonderful play that represents the life of Christ, but set in modern times, so I think we are all going to have a wonderful time rehearsing and preparing. I will see you all Wednesday evening during adult services. Auditions will be held in the church gymnasium." She looked at her watch then clapped her hands twice. "You can go, and no reading the scripts during the sermon today. Show respect for Pastor Bailey."

Sarah jumped up from her seat and grabbed her sweater and purse off the back of her chair. She would never think about disrespecting Pastor Bailey that way. Besides, Mrs. Bailey, his wife, was another person in church that Sarah admired and loved. She gently rolled her script and tucked it into her large handbag. Out of sight, out of mind.

She left the classroom and headed upstairs to the small auditorium where morning services were held. On her way, she glanced at the plain white clock over the main entrance. Services wouldn't start for another ten minutes; she had time to go see grandma before they began.

Fellow members of the small congregation were milling about, shaking hands and taking advantage of the time to tell each other hello. Sarah took no notice of them, rather she simply wove her way through the shaking hands and laughing faces until she reached her grandmother and the piano she had been playing for twenty years.

Sarah stopped about five feet from her grandmother, who was sitting on her wood bench and sorting sheet music for the hymns they would sing that morning. Watching her, Sarah felt a rush of warm love that made her shiver. A smile spread across her face, and she tiptoed until she was right behind the silver-haired woman. Letting her purse and sweater drop to the floor, she used her hands and covered her grandma's eyes.

"Guess who," she said in a low, gruff voice.

Grandma put on a big show, pretending to be confused. Her hands dropped from her sheet music, dramatically. "Oh, dear! That voice doesn't sound familiar at all. Let me see… Mayor Hendrix?"

"Nope," Sarah replied.

Now grandma gave a large sigh. "Oh, that's right. Mayor Hendrix doesn't come to church, does he? How about Walter Everman?"

Sarah couldn't pretend or hold back her giggles

anymore. She took her hands away and sat on the bench next to the regal-looking old woman. "It's me, goofy, and you knew it!"

Emma Holt took an exaggerated gasp. "No, no! You had me fooled! I could have sworn you were Walter Everman. You know he likes me." Her eyes twinkled, and she grinned. Then, she wrapped her arms around Sarah and gave her a big hug.

Sarah hugged her back and said, "Walter Everman? Yuck, Grandma. Stop teasing!"

"So, are you going to try out for Mary, or Elizabeth?" Emma asked.

Sarah shrugged and got a faraway look in her eyes. "I was thinking Mary Magdalene. She was one of Jesus' favorites, you know."

"Well, depending on who gets the part of Jesus anyway, right?" Emma batted at Sarah's head with some sheet music. "I know you are hoping that Brian Brandt gets it."

"Grandma, you're awful!" Sarah stood up and picked up her sweater and bag. The others in the church were nearly all seated, and the noise was dying down to a low rumble. "I'm getting a seat. See you after?"

"Yep. We'll stop for brunch on the way home." Emma turned her cheek toward her granddaughter and tapped it with her forefinger. "Plant one on me!"

Sarah gave her a peck and made her way to her favorite pew. It was second from the front on the left side. When she located her mother's face, she smiled and headed over to sit down.

"Dad couldn't come again?" Sarah asked.

Amelia Hathaway rubbed her daughter's shoulder and kissed her cheek. "They don't care if they work him to death, you know. I wish he would be more assertive with his supervisors when it comes to church, at least once a week. How's my mother? I saw you up there teasing her."

"Amazing," Sarah replied, "She wants me to have brunch with her after services."

"Why am I never invited to these things?" Amelia asked.

Sarah shrugged and smirked. "I'm her favorite."

Emma Holt began playing the prelude music, signifying that services were ready to start. The small congregation went quiet, and Pastor Bailey stood from where he had been praying from the altar and made his way to his podium with his bulky frame. With his Bible in hand, he positioned himself and held up his arms. The piano music stopped.

"It is God's wonderful blessing and provision that we are all here today, able to worship Him freely and come to Him together," He lowered his arms and gave a million-dollar smile. "Let us pray…"

∞

"I'm all set, Grandma!" Sarah had put on her jacket and slung her purse over her shoulder.

Emma stood, sheet music in hand, to put them in the bench and close up the piano. She stumbled just a bit, as she did so, but caught herself on the edge of the large instrument. "Whoo," she said, "Must have stood up too fast."

"Well, slow down," Sarah replied.

Emma began putting her jacket on. "I was hoping to talk you into coming to my place after brunch. I could use a bit of help with the walk. The neighbor used his snow-blower on my drive, but he and his wife had to leave for church. Will you shovel?"

"Absolutely." Sarah reached out and helped her grandma with her suit jacket. She noticed beads of sweat on Emma's forehead, and she looked a bit pale. "Are you okay, Grandma?"

Emma grasped the handle of her tote bag and smiled, waving the question away. "Of course. Why don't you grab my coat from the foyer closet?"

Sarah did as she was asked, and they left the church arm in arm. The small gravel parking lot had been cleared prior to church, and there was salt on the steps. They took their time, both chatting about the upcoming Christmas play.

∞

Brunch was wonderful, even though they did more talking than eating. There was only one restaurant in Paradise, Ohio, and nearly everyone in their congregation ate there on Sundays. It was called 'Evie's Eatery,' and it was filled with joy and laughter almost all the time.

When they both were finished enjoying their meals, Emma paid, and they headed to her house. It was only five blocks away, and they were there in no time. Emma parked her Buick in the garage, and they both climbed out of the car.

"You know where the shovel is, dear," Emma said with a point of her finger, "I'm going to collect garbage from around the house and put it in the can for the garbage man in the morning."

Sarah took the snow shovel and went out to the front yard. The walk was so covered in the snow she wouldn't have been able to see it at all if not for the small front porch and steps. She dug her shovel in and got to work.

It was cold out, but the sun was shining brightly. As Sarah shoveled, she lifted her face to its light and allowed it to energize her. The walk was cleared in fifteen minutes, so she headed back to the garage to put away the shovel and grab the bag of salt. She didn't want grandma falling, so better safe than sorry.

She crossed the yard and took a left into the drive. She hummed "In the Garden" as she walked, her favorite church hymn, and she looked at her feet as she went. When she looked back up, she saw two black plastic garbage bags lying on the ground near the garage. They looked pretty full to her. Had Grandma tossed those out for her to put in the can?

"Grandma!" she yelled, looking up to the kitchen window as she passed. She got no response, even though the old woman's hearing was quite good. "Never mind!" she yelled again. She would just put the bags in the can.

She approached the bags, and when she got about ten feet from them, she saw it: her grandmother was lying face down, and her small body was nearly concealed by the garbage bags. She wasn't moving.

"Grandma?" Sarah dropped the shovel and ran to her, kicking the bags out of her way. She grabbed the woman's frail body and turned her over. Emma's eyes were wide open, and Sarah could tell she was gone.

"Help! Help me!" She began to shake her grandma in panic. "No! Somebody call the ambulance!"

CHAPTER 2

"Dr. Martin, you have a call on line one."

The voice on the intercom seemed tinny, and it made Sarah's ears hurt like fingernails on a chalkboard. She sat in a chair in the waiting room at Mercy General Hospital, her eyes wet and her heart aching. Her mother sat next to her sobbing silently, but Sarah felt too frozen to cry.

Emma Holt had suffered a stroke in her driveway. Sarah knew there was nothing that could be done, but her mind wouldn't allow her to accept it. She called her mother and then rode in the ambulance with Grandma to the hospital. After Mother arrived, they were given the news: the stroke had been fatal.

That had been a half-hour ago, and they still sat there trying to wrap their minds around their loss. One of the nurses had gotten in touch with Pastor Bailey, and he and his wife would be there any minute. Sarah knew her mother couldn't drive them home in her state; the Baileys would take them.

Sarah put her head in her hands. She had not been able to cry yet, but she knew she would. She just held her own head and beat herself up. She should have made her grandma leave the trash for her. She shouldn't have allowed it. She should have done it first. In her mind, it was all her fault.

"Amelia? Sarah?" The two looked up immediately to see the pastor and his wife standing before them with stricken looks on their faces. Miriam Bailey had been crying, and her husband looked grieved.

Sarah stood up and ran to the woman, nearly falling into her waiting arms. Tears began to flow freely from her eyes then, as if the presence of the pair who had been such good friends to Emma Holt had brought her out of her trance.

"Cry it out, dear," Miriam whispered as she stroked the fifteen-year-old girl's blonde hair, "God knows. It's okay. Cry it out."

Sarah did. She wept non-stop for the next twenty minutes, long after the pastor had taken a seat next to her mother and put an arm of comfort around her. She completely lost touch with her surroundings until, finally, she looked up into Miriam's tear-filled eyes and said, "It was my fault. I shouldn't have let her do the trash. It was my fault."

"Sarah, no!" the woman replied softly. "Remember, all of our days are in the Lord's book. It was just her time, dear. It was just her time."

Miriam led the girl over to where her husband sat with Amelia Hathaway, who was drying her tears with a tissue from a box on her lap. Sarah reached over and took a couple for herself and blew her nose.

"I would like to pray with you both," Pastor Bailey

said, "For strength and grace."

They all took hands, and the pastor led the prayer, which Sarah hardly heard a word of. Afterward, they left the hospital to go home. The girl knew there would have to be arrangements, and as Emma Holt's only child, Amelia would have to deal with them.

"I got in touch with Kent at work," Mrs. Bailey said as they left the hospital parking lot, "He should be at your house by the time we get there."

Kent Hathaway was Sarah's father. He worked two jobs every day, and while Sarah loved him dearly, she hardly knew him, at least not like she knew her mother and grandmother. But she knew that her mother would need him now.

"Thank you," Amelia said, "I have been in such shock for the last hour I haven't been able to think straight."

"Understandable," Pastor Bailey replied, "This is never an easy time for anyone, Amelia."

Her mother turned and looked out the window, and Sarah did the same. She didn't want to talk, and she knew her mom didn't either. The silence was best for them right now.

They pulled into the driveway at the Hathaway home and parked behind her father's car. "Would you like us to come in?" Miriam asked.

Amelia offered her a weak smile of gratitude and squeezed the woman's arm gently. "No, we'll be fine."

"If you need anything, anything at all, you'll let us know?"

She nodded. "Right away."

Sarah and her mother got out and went into their home, where Kent Hathaway was pacing the floor and looking visibly shaken. When they came in, he held his arms out. "What happened?"

"Oh, Kent!" Her mother ran to him, dropping her purse on the kitchen floor. She flung herself into his arms and began to weep once more.

Sarah stood frozen by the kitchen door, her eyes glued on her mother's spilled bag. She didn't think she could move, so she leaned against the wall and slid down to the floor, where she began to silently let her tears fall again.

She was so glad things like this didn't happen every day; so glad.

∞

The next several days were a very difficult time for the Hathaway family. Grieving had to come in second to all the arrangements her mother and father were making. Sarah spent most of her time talking to her best friend. She and Michelle Karas had known each other practically since birth, and there was nothing one wouldn't do for the other. Michelle walked to her home every day and spent time in Sarah's room as her crying shoulder.

The Christmas play was canceled, and Sarah's parents kept her out of school for an entire week. Michelle brought her assignments when she would come in the afternoon, but Sarah had no motivation whatsoever. Everything reminded her of her grandma, even algebra.

"Michelle, why do you suppose He had to take her?" It was the first time Sarah had brought up the Lord's hand in things. Michelle could tell by the tone of her voice that she had a bit of anger at the Creator.

"We all die, Sarah," she replied softly. "Your grandma is with Jesus now."

Sarah snorted a laugh through her tears. "Yeah."

"Don't say that!" Her friend sat forward and looked into her eyes. "You know that is true. If you're mad at Him tell Him, but don't give him the cold shoulder."

That conversation stayed with Sarah for the rest of the week, and by the time the funeral came and went, she was in agreement with the words. It would do no good to get mad at God. She prayed through it, and by the time she went back to school the following Monday, she had pulled herself together quite well. With the exception of her broken heart, of course.

She would live, but she didn't want to go through those circumstances again any time soon.

R.W.K. Clark

CHAPTER 3

Sarah had been brought up in the church and, for as long as she could remember, attended youth groups and prayer meetings. If one of the congregation followers fell sick or had another passing. It was not unusual for members of the church family to surround the person or family and lay hands on them. As they implored the Lord God to move on that person or family's behalf. Up until the death of her Grandma Holt, Sarah had never questioned anything about her life.

To her, 'God and His miracles' were as real as someone standing in front of her.

But the recent occurrence and the death of her grandmother sent her into a spiritual tailspin that she didn't know was possible to experience. For the first three months following Grandma Holt's death, she kept her feelings of anger and doubt toward her Creator to herself. Out of anger, she even cursed him when she was alone, and though it frightened her to do such, she felt as though she would not survive if she didn't let this unseen deity know her true feelings.

Her best friend, Michelle, kept Sarah in her prayers constantly after Emma Holt died, as did the rest of the church. Sarah made no effort to hide her feelings of betrayal and rage; at least, she didn't in the initial months after the tragedy.

Slowly but surely, Sarah began to let go of things. Michelle had been right: everyone dies. With the passage of time, Sarah even realized how selfish it was to expect the God of the universe to allow her grandmother to be the only person in the history of the world to be immortal.

No, she knew she could not go on that way.

While she had avoided her grandmother's grave like the plague, in the beginning, she began to thaw somewhat, and that likely played the biggest part in her getting back to normal. The ice in her soul did melt, slowly but surely, and by the following April, the sting of Emma Holt's departure began to fade, little by little, a bit at a time.

The second influence on her road to recovery was her dog. Mitzi was a border collie that was as smart as a human being, and far, far more devoted and loyal. During the long nights when Sarah either couldn't sleep or would wake up with her body covered in sweat, her face covered in tears, she would open her eyes and Mitzi would be there. The dog would lick her tears and nuzzle the girl's neck until she was able to get a grip on reality.

Sarah loved that dog more than she liked many human beings, and she was grateful beyond measure for the companionship and seeming compassion that the pooch gave her.

On a breezy and warm spring morning at the beginning of the month, Sarah leashed the loving hound up and walked with her to Michelle's house for a long talk and some sincere apologies. Up to that morning, Sarah had been very self-involved; her grief would not let up, and she had been hateful to her life-long friend more than once. But she knew that the girl had continued her steadfast prayers, and she also knew that she would have to tell the girl how sorry she was for her behavior.

This admittance had come nearly overnight. Why, just the day before she had thought she surely wasn't going to make it through her tragedy alive, but when she woke on this morning, the sun shining through the slit in the curtains and kissing her face, she felt hope. She felt energized, and she began to see the light at the end of the tunnel.

So, Sarah walked with Mitzi, humming to herself and holding her face to the sun. After about ten minutes she stopped. She stood at the end of the long sidewalk that ended at Michelle Karas' front door, and she pondered her words. It wasn't like this was the first time the two had been together since her grandmother died. No, quite the contrary. Michelle had just visited her at home yesterday and took Sarah by the hands and prayed for her perseverance.

But it was the first time in a long time that she felt good enough to get past the pain, and she was at a loss as to how to put it all into words. Finally, after only a couple of minutes, Sarah shrugged in frustration and began to walk up the sidewalk to the house.

She had not even reached the door when it flung open. There stood Michelle in Capri jeans and a pink t-shirt that read 'Paradise Church of Christ… Support our Missions'. She was smiling, and a bit flushed as if she were excited.

"Sarah!" her friend stepped out onto the porch and closed the front door behind her, "It's… it's been a bit since you visited over here. How are you today?"

Sarah smiled and looked at her feet. She began to push a pebble around with the toe of her flip-flops. "Actually, I'm pretty darned good," she replied. "Maybe it's the sun."

Michelle came toward her quickly and wrapped her friend in an affectionate hug before stepping back and looking Sarah over. "No," the girl said. "I think the Lord pulled you through this. I knew that He would. I just knew it." She hugged her again with gusto. "Do you want to come in?"

"Actually, I thought that if you weren't doing anything you could walk with Mitzi and me up to Holy Cross Park. I haven't played with her much at all." She held up Mitzi's favorite green tennis ball. "It's time, I think."

Michelle's smile grew larger. "Sure! Let me just tell my mom and put on some shoes, okay?"

Sarah nodded, and Michelle went into the house. She looked around her friend's yard and smiled just a bit. Yes, this was just what she needed to do. She needed to pull herself up by her bootstraps and get back into her life once more, just as Grandma Holt was so fond of saying.

The door to the house opened after less than a minute, and Michelle reappeared, bouncing down the front steps. Her mother stood in the doorway behind her, a loving smile on her face. She was drying her hands on a dishtowel.

"You look wonderful, Sarah," she said. "Come up here and give me a hug before you two head off."

Sarah handed the end of Mitzi's leash to Michelle and shyly climbed the three steps of the porch. Carol Karas embraced her warmly as if she were her own daughter, then held her out at arm's length and looked her in the eye. "We have missed you, dear."

"Me too, Mrs. Karas," Sarah said.

The woman stepped back in a gesture that said, "You two scoot." She waved her hands to tell them to go. "Have fun, girls."

"We will, Mom," Michelle said, and the two girls headed down the sidewalk with Mitzi.

Holy Cross Park was only a couple of blocks from Michelle's house, so the girls strolled at a leisurely pace. There was no hurry; it was Saturday, after all, and both Sarah's mother and Mrs. Karas were so pleased that Sarah was going out that they offered no restrictions or complaints.

"So, you are better," Michelle observed, "What's different?"

Sarah shrugged a bit. "I don't know. I just woke up,

and the sun was shining, and things seemed...
different." She glanced at her friend and smiled. "I just
figured it was all the prayers, you know."

"See?" Michelle replied. "God knows. He's patient,
and he gave you the time you needed."

They arrived at the park and made their way to the
chain-link enclosure that served as the dog area. Sarah
was pleased to see that there were no other pets there,
only a few little kids and their mothers. She closed the
gate to the dog run and took Mitzi's leash off.

"Wanna play ball?" she asked the dog, waving the
tennis ball around in the air, "Does Mitzi wanna play
ball?" She gave the small orb a throw, and Mitzi
bounded off after the ever-elusive toy.

Michelle plopped down on the grass and settled in.
"The sun feels so good," she said, "Thanks for coming
to get me."

Mitzi bounded back with the ball and dropped it at
Sarah's feet. She picked it up and gave it another good
throw. "Wouldn't be the same without you," she
replied. "Listen, Michelle, I want you to know how
sorry I am for the way I have treated you since
Grandma died."

The girl lay down on the grass and blocked the sun
with her hand so she could see Sarah. "What do you
mean, how you have treated me?"

"You know," she continued, "I have been a bit...
rude, and I haven't been a good friend at all, but you
have."

Now the girl sat up once again. "Sarah, your

grandmother died. If I were worried about small, temporary things like that, I wouldn't have any friends at all. I mean, it was nothing personal, and I knew that."

Mitzi brought the ball again, and Sarah gave it another throw. "Thanks, but I really am sorry."

Once the words were said, Sarah felt as if a huge load had been taken from her, and she relaxed in her friend's presence. The two joked and laughed, and Michelle took a turn throwing Mitzi's ball.

Sarah had skipped church in recent months; oh, she had gone to the main services, but she had avoided her Sunday school classes altogether, and now she asked about her classmates, and Michelle was more than willing to fill her in.

When she was done, Sarah said, "I'm going back to Sunday school tomorrow."

She expected Michelle to put on a big, dramatic scene to show her encouragement, but the girl simply said, "Good. Everyone will be so glad to see you."

They hung out at the park for forty-five minutes; then, Sarah put Mitzi's leash back on. "I'm kinda hungry. Are you ready?"

With a nod from Michelle, the two girls and the dog left the park, laughing and talking. Michelle invited her for lunch and Sarah gladly accepted. She would call her mother and let her know when they got to Michelle's.

Yes, she would make it through alright.

∞

Sunday morning came quickly, and even though she was a bit nervous, Sarah was looking forward to seeing her friends, and she was looking forward to the services as well.

That was the second day of the rest of Sarah Hathaway's life. She found the strength to pick up where she had left off when Grandma Holt died, and she even found her faith again, though the fact of the matter was that she had never truly lost it. She had been genuinely hurt and angry that the God, she had always been told loved her, would take her grandma, but now those emotions seemed distant and surreal.

School ended the third of June, and Sarah said goodbye to the tenth grade with gusto. She and Michelle joined the girls' division of the church's summer softball league, and life went on.

∞

The second game of the season fell on a Saturday during the third week of June, and Sarah was anxious to play. They would be going up against Mary's Episcopal girls, and both Sarah and Michelle looked forward to it. During the first game of the year, they had won, and the confidence of the girls' team soared. If they came out on top, their team would be treated to a camping trip at Yosemite National Park at the end of the year, and it was a very big deal. So far Sarah felt pretty good about their chances, even if they had played only one game.

"Sarah!" Amelia Hathaway yelled from the foot of the stairs. "You need to eat before you leave for your game. It's time to get a move on, girl!"

Sarah bounded from her bedroom with Mitzi at her heels. She had her leather glove on one hand; a softball was nestled in it. She wore her red and white Paradise Powderpuffs uniform, and her red cap sat backward on her head.

She took the stairs two at a time. She could smell bacon and scrambled eggs, and her stomach growled. Her father, Kent, sat at the table with the paper open and a steaming cup of coffee in front of him. He glanced up at her and smiled as she sat at her place at the table.

"Planning another victory, I see," he teased as her mother placed a glass of milk and a plate of food before her daughter.

Sarah removed her glove and set it, with the ball, next to her chair on the floor. "Of course. It wouldn't be fun if teams didn't plan to win."

Her father chuckled. "Well, your mother and I are going to an auction in Canton, and we will be there most of the day, as you know. If you don't want to worry about Mitzi needing to go outside, you might want to take her and leash her up inside the dog run at the park."

Sarah looked over at the brown-eyed border collie and smiled as the dog thumped its tail against the floor. She looked at Sarah with pleading eyes, as if to say 'Please take me!'

"I wouldn't want it any other way," she replied, "Well, Mitzi, it looks like you need to get ready to make a day of it."

Amelia Hathaway said, "I'll pack up a baggie of kibble and a couple of treats. You make sure she gets enough water to drink."

Sarah nodded as she chewed a mouthful of food, then swallowed and replied. "There is a water trench for the dogs in the run. She'll be fine." She looked back at Mitzi and said in her best baby voice, "You wanna go, don'tcha? Yes, you do!"

Breakfast went fairly quickly, as Sarah wasted no time in getting her food down. She was anxious to hit the park and get warmed up. She wiped her mouth on her napkin and stood up. "I better get going. I'm stopping for Michelle on the way, and it won't do to be late to the game."

"The dog food is in your duffle bag," her mother said, "You'll be home before us, so you'll have to make your lunch. There are frozen pizzas in the deep freeze. That should tide you over."

Sarah gave both of her parents a hug and kiss, then put the leash on Mitzi before swinging the duffle bag over her shoulder. "I'm outta here!"

The day was beautiful, with a bright, shining sun and a clear blue sky. Flowers had sprung up brightly in seemingly every flower bed in the neighborhood. "What do you think of this day, girl? I don't think it could be more perfect." Mitzi barked in response.

Sarah held her leash in her left hand, and she wore her baseball glove on the right, with her softball in the pocket. As she walked, she talked to her dog, who always answered right on cue, and with each bark, Sarah would toss the softball into the air and catch it in the mitt. She looked both ways before crossing the next intersection; Michelle's house was three houses down on the other side of the street. As she made it to the other side, she told the dog, "Almost there, girlie! Almost there."

Mitzi gave another excited bark as they approached the end of Michelle's front sidewalk. Sarah gave the softball one final toss into the air, and it wasn't until she attempted to catch it that she realized her toss was way off course. Without being aware, she let go of Mitzi's leash just long enough to shoot forward to catch it, but she missed.

The ball hit the curb directly and bounced once before rolling out into the street. Mitzi shot into the street to fetch, her leash dragging behind her. The dog was compelled to fetch any getaway ball there was.

"Mitzi, no!" Sarah hollered sharply, but it was too late. The next thing she heard was the deafening squeal of tires and a soft thud, both of which were followed by the pained yelp of her dog. "Mitzi!"

Sarah threw the glove onto the ground and dropped her duffle bag as she ran to her beloved pet. Mitzi lay motionless under the front passenger tire of a pickup truck, blood pooled around her head, which Sarah could not see.

"No! Oh, Mitzi!"

She dropped to her knees with sobs next to her animal. Tears blinded her eyes, and she didn't even notice that the driver of the truck was standing next to where she knelt, as her head was buried in the dog's side. Mitzi was not breathing.

"I... I... I'm so sorry," the young man said with wide, pained eyes. "It came out of nowhere. I'm so sorry."

Sarah began to shake her dog. "Mitzi, wake up!" She turned to the driver then, hysterical. "Your tire is on her head! It's on her head!"

The driver got back into the truck to back it up just as Michelle came running. "Oh, my Lord!" She knelt down next to her best friend, who was completely unaware of her presence.

The truck backed up a couple of feet finally to reveal the bloodied border collie. It was like something from a bad dream.

Suddenly the world began to swim, and Sarah Hathaway passed out cold in the street.

CHAPTER 4

Sarah woke with a start and sat straight up. The room she was in was very dark. Only after her eyes adjusted to the moonlight coming in through a window, did she realize she was in her own room. How did she get there? Did they win the softball game? She couldn't even remember playing.

She looked at the alarm clock on her nightstand. It was ten-thirty at night. Had she been dreaming that she had a game to go to? Sarah struggled to line her thoughts up with reality, and that was when it all came back to her, like a flood of knife wounds in the chest and gut.

Mitzi…

Her stomach sunk to her feet and she quickly swung her legs over the side of her bed. She was suddenly overcome with vertigo; heat tore through her body, and her hands began to tremble violently. What's going on?

"Mom! Dad!" she cried out, "Somebody!"

Sarah heard footsteps pounding up the hallway through her fog. The bedroom door flew open, and light flooded her room. Her mother and father were standing in the doorway, stricken looks on their faces.

Her mother ran to her and sat on the bed. She pulled her daughter into her arms. "I'm here, baby. Mother is here."

"Where is Mitzi?" she asked, looking up into her mother's face.

Amelia looked to her husband as she struggled with her words. Kent stepped all the way into the room and approached them. He then knelt before his daughter and said, "You should lie back down, Sarah."

Sarah turned to him, her eyes flashing. "Where's Mitzi?"

Kent breathed a labored sigh and looked down at the floor. "She had an accident. Do you remember?"

Sarah nodded. "But where is she, daddy?"

"She's gone, honey. We had to bury her." Tears welled up in his eyes as he continued. "I made a nice marker for her grave. You can visit her tomorrow if you like."

Now Sarah began to struggle against her mother's embrace. She jerked away violently and stood up so, she could face them both. "No. You're lying." Her voice was frighteningly still and controlled.

Neither of the Hathaways answered their daughter; they simply held her gaze as her mind struggled to wrap around the truth. After only a few minutes, the girl crumpled to the floor with great sobs. Kent and Amelia both sat down on the floor in silence to give her the support she needed.

After about ten minutes, Sarah stilled a bit and drew a tired breath. So, now God saw fit to take Mitzi away too. This God was nothing like she had been taught. He was cruel and cold, playing painful tricks for his own amusement. She didn't know if she could handle being His jester for long.

"Where is she buried?" she asked quietly.

Kent cleared his throat and squeezed her shoulder gently. "She's out back. You can see where tomorrow after church if you like, but for now you need to go back to bed, dear."

Sarah jumped to her feet, stumbled from dizziness for a second, then got her balance. "Church? Ha! I won't be going to church." She stumbled again, and her mother had to grab her to keep her from falling. "Why am I so dizzy?"

Her mother guided her to her bed and helped her sit down. "Dr. Martin had to give you something for your nerves, honey. You were hysterical, and you needed help to calm down. He said it would make you dizzy when you woke."

"I want to see her grave now."

"Sarah, you need to–," Kent began.

"Now!"

Kent's face went stony as Amelia said, "Maybe it wouldn't hurt, dear."

He turned to his wife. "What, and have to call Dr. Martin over here to tranquilize her again? No," he said as he turned to his daughter, "You will wait for tomorrow, whether you go to church or not." With that he walked out of the room to leave the two alone, closing the door softly behind him.

Sarah and her mother sat in silence for a bit. After only a few moments, the girl lay back onto the bed, and she allowed Amelia to pull the blankets up over her. Sarah's eyes were cold and angry.

"Honey, it's okay to be mad at God," she began, "but don't let your anger keep you away from Him. He knows you are angry, and He knows how you feel."

Sarah shot her mother a look of fury. "I don't even want to think about Him."

"That's fine," Amelia concluded, "But, for tonight, you need to get some more rest. You may find you have a new perspective in the morning, okay?"

The girl did not respond, and Amelia threw her hands in the air mentally. She bent over her daughter and kissed her cheek. "I'm going to let you be alone. Call me if you need me."

The woman left the room to join her husband, shutting the light off behind her. Sarah lay on her bed in the darkness, and she was fuming. So, her parents expected her to continue on to church, the house of the God that was betraying her like nothing had happened, as if He had done nothing. No, she wouldn't have it.

But she knew that wouldn't fly for long. They would make her return for her own good, to act appropriately in her relationship with Him. She already knew, and her father may even make her go in the morning.

She finally started to doze off, and the last thought she had was, "I have a lot of pretending to do."

∞

Sarah Jean Hathaway knew there was a God, or at

least she thought she did.

The fact of the matter was that she wasn't quite ready to write Him off completely. After all, she had been raised in the church. If He wasn't real, how could she be angry at Him? No, he was real, and Sarah was pissed, but her anger began to fade once again.

Like Michelle was so fond of saying, everybody dies.

Surprisingly, she began to heal from the loss of Mitzi much faster than when her grandmother passed, and it surprised her. Oh, her anger and disappointment in the Lord were still there. She went to church every Sunday begrudgingly, and she had her doubts that floated through her mind and tugged at her sense of reason, but having Michelle Karas for a friend really helped her, both spiritually and emotionally. She was glad to have a best friend like Michelle.

So the summer continued. Even with her softball team losing the second game after Mitzi's death, they still took the regional trophy. The two girls participated together, thanks to Michelle's encouragement, and toward the end of July, Sarah found that the game kept her focus off her broken heart.

While she went to church, Sarah was still doubtful, but she continued to read her Bible and pray. She and Michelle would even pray together when they were alone, and it too helped. Once again, the pain faded, and she knew she would make it.

∞

One Saturday toward the end of July, after softball league was over, Sarah and Michelle decided to go spelunking at the caves on the outskirts of town. The caves were only about two miles from town, and the girls decided to pack lunches and ride their bikes. Neither could wait until the following year when their parents would allow them to study to obtain their driver's licenses, but in the meantime, they would enjoy what they had.

They planned the outing for three weeks. They wanted to do it the week after the championship softball game, which the Paradise Powderpuffs won. It would be a celebration of sorts, and they were both looking forward to some quality time alone.

Sarah had not spoken to Michelle for much of the week, but she thought nothing of it. She knew that her friend volunteered at a local nursing home often, so when she didn't call, Sarah simply assumed she was working. On Friday evening she called Michelle only to make sure that their plans were still a go, and Michelle had reassured her that they were. They agreed to meet at Holy Cross Park and ride to the caves from there.

∞

Now it was Saturday morning, and Sarah was ready to go, her lunch packed and her tires full of air. It was going to be a great day.

Just as planned, the two girls met up and set out for the caves. They chatted along the way, but Sarah felt a vibe coming from her friend that was abnormal. She didn't participate in the conversation the way she usually did. If Sarah cracked a joke, Michelle hardly laughed at all. Her friend exuded a tension that was tangible.

When they got to the caves, they chained their bikes to a tree at the park entrance and started their hike. It was sunny, and there was a light breeze that seemed to push the heat away from them. Sarah loved the caves, and she was eager to explore, even if they had done this fifty times before. Michelle liked them too, but today she wasn't herself.

The girls had a routine. They would explore the smaller caves toward the front of the park, then they would stop for lunch before hitting the last two caves, which were the largest and most fun. By the time they were ready to eat lunch, Sarah felt frustrated. It was time to confront her friend regarding her mood.

They found a picnic table and began to unpack their lunches. When Sarah was finished, she popped a can of soda and said, "Michelle, what's wrong with you today?"

Her friend looked at her, and Sarah could see that she was struggling. "Tell me."

Tears began to fall down Michelle's face all of a sudden. "My dad got laid off this week," she said once she caught her breath.

Sarah immediately reached out to comfort her sobbing friend. "Oh, no!" she replied, "What happened?"

"It was nothing he did," Michelle said, "Rickson Securities laid off a bunch of workers from this location."

Sarah began to stroke her friend's arm. "I'm sorry. He'll find something soon, I know it. Maybe my dad can get him in down at the lab, or maybe at the packing plant where he works at night."

Michelle looked down at her food, avoiding Sarah's eyes. She pretended to arrange the meat and cheese on her sandwich, but Sarah saw that the sandwich stayed the same. Finally, Michelle spoke in a quiet voice.

"Well, that's not going to work, you see."

Sarah knit her brow. "What do you mean? Your dad and mom have bills to pay, just like my parents. It certainly couldn't hurt."

Now Michelle looked her in the eye. "He already has a job. It's still with Rickson Securities, though, and it's a different position; it pays much more."

Sarah's face lit up. "That's awesome! See, there is no problem, Michelle. It will be alright."

Michelle stood up and began to pace before her friend, her lunch forgotten. "The new position is at the headquarters. It's in California."

The smile fell from Sarah's face immediately. "You mean you're moving?"

Her friend stopped and looked at her, nodding her head slowly. "I don't want to move away, Sarah. I mean, I've lived here my whole life, but I just don't have a choice."

Sarah's heart was pounding in her chest. Michelle move away? She felt so sick she wanted to throw up.

"We can pray" Michelle finally said, "We can ask God to bring him a job that is just as good as the one in California. God won't pull us apart, I know He won't."

Tears were spilling from Michelle's eyes, and Sarah's were puddling up in her own eyes. "Yeah, maybe that will work," Sarah replied, "We should pray every single day until the move. Maybe God will intervene. Can we pray right now?"

Sarah nodded, and Michelle sat back down. The two girls held hands, and with bowed heads and closed eyes. They began to ask the God of the universe to intervene on their behalf, to bring lucrative employment to either Carol or Rick Karas or both of them, so they could stay in Paradise.

For the next week, the two girls prayed furiously. They prayed every morning on the phone together. They prayed in the afternoon at Holy Cross Park after lunch. They prayed again on the phone before bed at night, and after they hung up, Sarah would pray herself to sleep.

He would help, Sarah told herself. He would make a way for the girls to stay together. But no matter how many times she told herself, that great doubt continued to flood her soul, and she knew in her heart of hearts that He would do nothing. She just refused to quit.

∞

The following Friday, the day before Michelle and her family planned to set out for California, came all too quickly. Both girls spent the entire week on edge, waiting, wishing, and hoping that the God they had worshipped all their lives would suddenly come down and wave a magic wand and 'Poof!' Rick Karas would have a job.

By Wednesday, they really began to sweat, and on Friday evening, they were both on the phone in their respective bedrooms sobbing hysterically. Nothing happened; no salvation came down from the sky. The Karas family was all packed, and they would be leaving at seven the following morning, leaving their house to be sold by Paradise Real Estate.

They spent as much time together that week as they could. They had asked their parents if Michelle could stay over for a night with Sarah, giving them more time together, and they received permission. Michelle ended up staying with Sarah on Tuesday night, but the quality time resulted in nothing more than greater sadness and a more intense sense of loss for them both. They stuck to phone calls for the rest of the week for their prayers and time together.

On the morning they were to leave, Sarah woke at quarter to five in the morning. She had no appetite, so she quickly dressed and left a note for her parents telling them she was going to see Michelle and her family off. She stepped outside to find cloudy skies and drizzling rain, and it made her feel more miserable than ever.

The goodbyes between them were stiff and painful. Michelle left her new address with Sarah so they could write, and she promised to call with their new number as soon as their phone was connected. They hugged and cried and hugged some more. Finally, Michelle and her younger brother climbed into their mother's minivan and left. Sarah stood in the rain waving while her tears fell and mixed with the drops of water on her face.

When they were finally out of sight, Sarah Jean Hathaway looked up at the sky with a sneer. "I really don't know how much more of this I can take, God."

With that, she walked home.

R.W.K. Clark

CHAPTER 5

With September came two events: Sarah's sixteenth birthday and the start of her junior year in high school. As time always proved her, sharp pain over Michelle's move dulled; though, she was a bit apprehensive over what it would be like to return to school without her best friend. A bitter melancholy seemed to follow her wherever she went, regardless of what she did.

So, Sarah dealt with it by diving into school. She became a cheerleader and began tutoring other kids. She joined the school paper and ran for student body president, a position which she did not get. She didn't care; she did it only to keep her mind off her pain.

With the onset of the school year, she became very withdrawn. The girl who had once been the life of the party suddenly had no desire to have attention, or even socialize. Boys asked her out, but she had no desire to accept. Who would she talk to about her dates? Her mother and father? No, she would simply thank the young men politely and decline.

She decided on a college major that year: she wanted to be a veterinarian, mostly in Mitzi's honor. She began to take classes which would support her goals, and she found that the additional study load acted as a sedative.

Sarah knew deep inside that she would never be the same.

The second week in October was a busy one for her. She stepped into the editor position for her class paper, and she set her focus on being the very best editor she could be. She started a series of articles about the ties between high school sports and traumatic brain injuries, and the research and interviews took much of her spare time. Overall, though, she thought she had found ways to survive the constant pain and inner turmoil she felt.

On October fifteenth, Sarah finished up her work early at school, and she made her way home. Usually, she would offer to stick around and help other students just to have company and keep from thinking too much, but on that day she felt very, very tired. The thought of staying any longer overwhelmed her, so she loaded her books into her backpack and headed for home.

∞

"Mom? Dad? I'm home," Sarah shouted as she flipped through the mail in the foyer. Still no letter from Michelle. She shook her head and tossed the small pile of envelopes back on the table. "Anyone here?"

She was met with no response, so she made her way to the kitchen for a snack. At the table sat her mother and father. "Didn't you two hear me when I came in?"

Kent Hathaway nodded at her, so she shifted her gaze to her mother. The woman's eyes were rimmed with red, and it was obvious she had been crying.

"Are you okay, Mom? What's wrong?" She dropped

her backpack into her chair at the table and made her way to her parents, but her dad stopped her in her tracks.

"Sarah, you should have a seat," he said.

She stopped abruptly and gave him a look of confusion, but she obeyed immediately. "What's up?" she asked as she moved her bag and sat down.

Kent cleared his throat. "Your mother and I have something to tell you."

Immediately Sarah's heart skipped a beat. With wide eyes she asked, "What is it? What's going on?"

Amelia shook her head and looked down at her hands, which she was fidgeting with in her lap. Kent reached out to comfort her and looked at his daughter. "Your mother had an appointment with Dr. Martin last week, and he sent her for some tests at the hospital," he began, "We went, and today we got the results of the tests. Your mother has been diagnosed with breast cancer."

Sarah could hear the crashing of waves in her head, and the floor seemed to drop out from under her. "Breast cancer?"

Kent nodded and continued. "Yes, and it is pretty far along."

"So what are they going to do?" she asked.

"Well, tomorrow she checks in for surgery," he said quietly as her mother sobbed, "They will do a double-mastectomy, and hopefully that takes care of it."

Amelia wiped her eyes and looked at her daughter. "All we can do is pray, Sarah. I am hoping you will; I know how rocky your relationship with the Lord has been for nearly a year, but this is in his hands."

Sarah stood. "Of course, Mom. Um, can I be excused to my room? I need to think for a moment."

"Go ahead, dear," her mother said, "Come down when you are ready."

Sarah grabbed her backpack and jogged out of the kitchen and up to her room. She threw the pack on the floor and slammed the door before collapsing onto her bed. Tears began to fall freely then, and she didn't fight them.

She cried into her pillow for a full twenty minutes, her mind racing. Finally, she rolled over onto her back and spoke to the sky. "God, I know I haven't been the easiest child. I have only been angry, but I need you now, my mom needs you now. I am begging you for your mercy."

She prayed the same words over and over, but they brought her no release, and Sarah ended up crying herself to sleep, her lips still moving. She slept for only an hour.

When she woke, she felt peaceful, and she decided to take that emotion as God's way of reassuring her that her mother was going to be okay. She needed to get as close to Him as possible right now. She needed to devote her time to prayer, both alone and with her parents. She would have her Sunday school class pray too.

She left her room and went into the bathroom, where she washed her face and brushed her hair, then she made her way to the kitchen. Her father sat alone at the table, an empty coffee cup in his hand. He was staring into space and didn't hear her enter.

"Where's Mom?" she asked.

Kent was jerked back to reality by the sound of his daughter's voice. "She's laying down for a bit. She has been pretty tired out lately."

Sarah sat down at the table. "We need to pray, daddy."

Kent gave his daughter a relieved smile. "That would be wonderful, Sarah."

The two held hands and prayed feverishly for the next half-hour. When they were done, Sarah let him know that she would be attending church without any hassle, and she was going to pray for her mother every chance she got and with anyone who would join her.

"We have to practice our faith now, daddy," she told him matter-of-factly.

He nodded. "I know it, kid. I just have to tell you that I'm scared. Not of death, but of losing your mother."

"I'm scared too," she told him, "But we have to do this now."

After they prayed, she stood up and headed to the sink. "I'll make supper tonight," she said, "We should let Mom sleep."

But a half-hour later, her mother came into the kitchen, where Sarah was busying herself with fried chicken. "Honey, I can do that if you like."

"No, Mom," she replied, "I have this. Why don't

you go be with Dad? I think he needs you now."

Amelia offered up a weak smile and turned to go. "Oh, Mom?" Sarah asked.

"Yes, dear?"

"What time is your surgery?"

Amelia gave her a small smile and a slight shrug. "Early in the morning," she said, then she left the kitchen.

When she was gone, Sarah turned back to the meal she was preparing, and she began to pray as she cooked. She would waste no time, for her mother had no time to waste. So, God didn't intervene when they prayed for Michelle to stay, but this was a life and death situation. If He were a God of love and mercy, he would surely spare the life of Amelia Hathaway.

Even as Sarah prayed, even as she wept quietly during her prayer, doubt tugged at her heart. After all she had gone through in the last year, how could she count on Him? She didn't know, but she knew she had no one else to turn to, so she had no choice.

When the meal was ready, the Hathaway family sat down and ate together quietly. The grace they offered for the food was filled with requests for mercy. When it was time to eat, none of them felt hungry. They were filled with tension and anxiety.

They were filled with fear.

∞

The next morning, Kent and Sarah sat in the waiting room at the hospital's surgical unit. They were both on edge, and it was all they could do to pray to God and try to have faith. Time would only tell if God was going to act or not, but Sarah had plenty of doubts, even as she prayed with her father.

Sarah prayed to herself mostly, and at that time, she began to bargain with God. She tried to make the best deal with Him she could. If He would heal her mother, she would devote the rest of her life to His service; if He would not, she would wash her hands of that relationship.

Once and for all.

R.W.K. Clark

CHAPTER 6

Sarah sat at the vanity in her bedroom staring at her tear-covered reflection. Her father was downstairs waiting on the Reverend and Mrs. Bailey to stop over for a visit. Her mother was still in the hospital, in post-surgery recovery. They had come home only to shower and eat, and while they were there, the Baileys had called. Her father was visibly relieved that they were coming, but Sarah didn't care one way or another. While she looked at herself, her mind flashed back to the hospital and the surgeon who had come out to talk to them.

"Your wife is in recovery now," he had said to her father as he sat in a chair next to them, "She made it through, but I'm afraid the prognosis isn't good."

As soon as he said those words, Sarah had shut down. Her father pressed the doctor for more details. "What do you mean, 'not good'?" He had asked.

The surgeon, a man named Dr. Trask, took a deep breath. "The double mastectomy was successful, but to be honest with you, her body is riddled with cancer. When it has metastasized in this manner, there is very little we can do." His voice was quiet, and his eyes were filled with compassion, but Sarah highly doubted that the emotion went any further than that.

"What does that mean?" Kent asked him, "If there is nothing you can do, then what are you doing now?"

Another deep breath. "All we can really do is keep her as comfortable as possible. I recommend that you find a quality hospice to come in and take over. I can point you in the direction of some very good ones if you'd like."

Sarah stared at her shoes, rage building up inside of her. "So how long?" Kent asked.

Dr. Trask looked sheepish, as though even he were disgusted with what he was about to say. "A month, maybe two at the very most, but I would say not that long, more than likely."

Sarah stood up and headed for the elevator without saying a word. She didn't want to hear anymore. She punched the down button over and over in an effort to make the car come faster. Tears ran down her face and burned her eyes, but other than that she looked mostly composed.

Finally it arrived, and she rode it down to the first floor. When she stepped out, she ran for the main entrance. She wanted out of there, as far away from the place as she could get, and as soon as possible. The large glass doors of the entrance swung open before her as if by magic, and she continued her pace until she was at her father's car. Almost as if on cue, she doubled over next to the passenger door and vomited, emptying her stomach completely.

When she was done, she stood upright and wiped her mouth with the back of her hand. The tears had stopped altogether, and nausea had disappeared as well. She looked around the parking lot; no one was around her, and she was relieved.

"Sarah."

Her father's voice came from behind her. She turned around and looked at him, her eyes flashing, and said nothing. He cleared his throat and kicked at an invisible rock.

"Your mother is still in recovery, and she isn't all the way awake yet," he said, "I thought we would go home and eat and clean up. Then we can come back up and see her. Are you okay?"

Now she offered him a snide laugh. "Do you think I'm okay? How okay are you?"

"Right," he replied, "Stupid question."

∞

Sarah sat at the vanity that her mother had picked out for her in the room that her mother had helped her to decorate. She was staring at a reflection that had her mother's eyes, and she wanted to scream.

"Well, God," she said simply, "Have it your way."

She heard the doorbell ring, and she knew that the Baileys had arrived. They were the last people she wanted to see, so she stayed in her room. She lay down on her bed with her back to the door and pretended to sleep; there was no way she was going to deal with God, or anyone representing Him, anymore.

The thought of going to see her mother made her

sick. She knew she would have to do it, for her mother's sake, but she certainly wasn't ready right now. What the heck did everyone expect from her, anyway? She had taken just about all she could take.

Sarah was worn out, physically and emotionally. As she lay on her bed cursing God, she started to doze off, but she was pulled out of her light slumber by a knock on her bedroom door.

"Sarah? It's Mrs. Bailey. Miriam."

Her eyes shot open, but she did not respond. "I just wondered if I could talk to you, just for a few minutes," Mrs. Bailey persisted.

Sarah swung her legs to the floor and went to unlock the door. When she opened it, Miriam Bailey stood there, her own eyes red with tears. "You've had a pretty bad year, haven't you honey?"

Sarah pretended she didn't hear the woman. She turned and walked back to her bed and sat down. Mrs. Bailey entered as well, her eyes fastened on Sarah's every move.

"I just wanted to know if you wanted to talk," Miriam said, "About anything; anything at all."

Sarah looked up at her with tired and disgusted eyes, but she did not reply. She simply held the woman's eyes wearily, as if to say, "Are you serious?"

At last Miriam looked away. "I guess not, huh? Well, can I pray for you then?"

"Absolutely not."

The tone of Sarah's voice shocked and surprised the pastor's wife, and it showed on her face. It took the woman a moment to gain her composure. "Sarah, you know God loves you. He wants to help you get through this, and everything else for that matter."

Now Sarah laughed, but it was bitter laughter. "I wouldn't need help at all if He hadn't taken away every last person or being that I love. It sounds like hogwash to me, so thanks, but no thanks."

Miriam Bailey audibly gasped at Sarah's contempt. "Sarah, I…"

The girl stood up and walked to her bedroom door, which she took hold of and held open. "I don't need a friend. I don't want prayer. I want to be alone, please."

Mrs. Bailey stood and looked at her for only a moment longer before walking slowly through the threshold. She turned to look at the girl; she wanted to tell her she would be there for her if she changed her mind, but Sarah slammed the door in her face. Miriam heard the lock click into place and then silence.

She made her way to the dining room where Kent Hathaway and Pastor Bailey were seated. Kent turned to look at the woman with eyes filled with concern. "What did she say?" he asked.

Miriam sat down across from her husband. "She's angry, Kent. She is very angry, and the anger is aimed at God."

"Did you pray with her?" he asked.

The woman shook her head. "No. She's not having it right now. Listen, it is going to be very important that you be patient with Sarah. She has gone through a tremendously painful year, as you said. If we push her, it will do nothing but compel her to draw further away."

Kent nodded and put his head in his hands. He began to cry in earnest. He was losing his wife; he did not want to lose his daughter too. "What do I do?"

Pastor Bailey patted him on the shoulder. "You are going to have to leave it in God's hands. Be there for her, but let Him do the work."

∞

Sarah and her father returned to the hospital early that evening to see Amelia Hathaway. When they had taken her to the hospital she looked tired, but she had been herself. This time, when they walked into her room, she looked tiny and sick. It was amazing what the disease had taken out of her in such a short amount of time.

Sarah was the first to hug and kiss her mother, then she stepped back to allow her father to be with his wife. Amelia Hathaway was terribly weak, so weak that she struggled to keep her eyes open. The nurse at the desk had warned them that she was on heavy doses of pain medication, and now Sarah could see that clearly. She simply watched as the shell of the woman that was her mother spoke to Kent.

"The doctor... said I don't have a lot of time," she whispered, "I'm glad because I hurt so much."

Kent stroked his wife's hand as tears fell from his eyes. "Yes, but not today, Amy. Not today. We still have time."

Amelia smiled, first at her husband, then at her daughter. "I don't want any more time."

It was all Sarah could take, and she turned and left the room quietly. There were two nurses at the desk, so she approached the nearest one. "Can you tell me where the chapel is?"

The woman looked up at her and offered her a sad smile. "Take the elevator to the second floor and go left when you get off. The signs will take you there."

"Thank you," she replied, as she turned to leave. She stopped short and turned back to the nurse. "If my father asks would you please tell him where I am?"

"No problem," the nurse said.

Sarah made her way to the elevator. If her father knew she went to the chapel, he would let her be. He was aware of her anger toward God, and all he wanted her to do was pray, but she had no intention of begging Him anymore. No, she was going to the chapel for other reasons.

She found it easily enough and turned the knob to the solid oak door. The chapel was dimly lit with fake candles, and there were six padded pews in the room, three on each side. At the front was an altar, and that was where she went.

She didn't kneel; instead, she stood at the altar and looked at a statue of Jesus which was situated on a small stage. He was kneeling, and he was looking up to heaven with grief in his eyes. Sarah recognized it as depicting Christ praying in the Garden of Gethsemane.

"You prayed to Him too, and He didn't help you out either, did He?" She continued to look at the statue as if waiting for it to answer. Finally, she said, "Well, if

He didn't help His own Son, I don't know why I ever thought He would do anything for me."

She crossed her arms over her chest and began to pace back and forth before the altar. She was thinking about what to say, for she wanted to choose her words wisely. She meant them, and she wanted Him to know it.

At last, she stopped and looked up at the ceiling. "I lived the way you wanted me to, but it wasn't enough. I must be one of the worst people on this God-forsaken planet for you to punish me the way you have. So I'm going to do you a favor; I'm severing this relationship. Don't call me, and I won't call you."

With that, she turned on her heel and left.

∞

By the time she got back to her mother's room, her mother had passed away. It had been quick and easy, though her father looked terribly haggard and depressed. The two of them sat in chairs in a visitors' lounge holding each other. Sarah had shut off her emotions, but her father needed her support.

"I thought Dr. Trask said at least a month," she said as she held Kent's hand.

He was crying, and he shrugged in the midst of his tears. "She wanted to go," he said, "I think she just wanted me to give her the 'all-clear.' She said she didn't want us to hurt over it; she is in Heaven where she is happy and well. That's all that matters."

Sarah stood up. "How can you even begin to make it sound as though being with God fixes anything? Tell me, do you really believe that He genuinely cares about anyone? If He is indifferent to our problems on Earth, can you honestly say you believe we can trust Him to take any of us to Heaven when we die?"

Her father snapped his eyes up at her. "Sarah, I won't have you talking this way about the Lord!"

She smirked and shook her head. "Lord this," she said, "I'll meet you at the car."

As she made her way to the parking lot, she felt as though she had made the best decision of her life.

R.W.K. Clark

CHAPTER 7

"That will be fourteen dollars and ninety-seven cents, please." Sarah offered up a smile to the elderly woman before her and waited for her to count the appropriate change. "Thank you. Have a nice day."

She had taken the job at Wonder Mart to help supplement her father's income. Since her mother passed four months ago, things had been pretty rough. Her dad worked at one job or another constantly. She went to school and now had a job herself, so it was a rare occasion if they ever got to see each other or spend quality time together.

The smiles she offered the customers each day only went as far as her face. Sarah had felt no real joy in so long that she was almost convinced that she was a robot. She didn't let herself think about any of the losses she had suffered; she almost had herself convinced that they all happened to someone else.

She held true to her promise to not step foot in a church again. Her father still attended regularly, but she wouldn't budge on her position no matter how often he tried to talk to her about it. Pastor Bailey had even tried to talk to her on a couple of occasions, but both attempts ended badly. She even had to get rude to him to make her stance clear. She was not going to church anymore. She was done.

She looked down at her watch: seven-thirty. She was finally off work and could clock out. She was anxious to go home and do her homework before bed, so she quickly shut down her register and took her smock off as she went to the breakroom to fetch her purse and backpack from her locker.

It was a short walk home, and she made it there in record time. Her father wasn't home yet, so she went to her room and began to empty out the contents of her backpack. That was when she remembered she had checked out a very special book from the library that day: 'Witches' Creed' by Francis Paducci. She stared at the cover and ran her hand over it, smiling.

After her mother died, she had done a lot of thinking about why God had forsaken her, and she came to a single conclusion: she was evil herself. When she had returned to school after the funeral, the other students had started to give her a hard time. They made fun of her quiet stance, her clothing, her makeup. Most of them were her old Sunday school classmates, and as hard as that was to believe, she wasn't surprised at all.

She hated them right back.

But last week had been particularly unbearable. When she was showering after gym, the other girls had begun to throw bars of soap at her, pelting her flesh with them. There had been no escape, and she had been humiliated beyond words. She had gone home and cried.

How could this be happening, she thought. She had gone to school with the same kids since her educational career had begun, and it was difficult to believe that all of them had turned on her the way they had. As she lay in her bed that night thinking about it, she could come up with only one solution: witchcraft. She would learn and curse them all.

So, today, she stopped at the public library on her way to work and found this book. It was simple for her to understand and offered a variety of beginner's spells which the author guaranteed would be simple, even for the youngest aspiring witch. Now she held the book in her hands and became entranced by it.

Sarah cleared the school books off her bed and sat down. She opened 'Witches Creed' to the first chapter and began to read. By the time she was three pages in, she was thoroughly convinced she had chosen the correct path for herself. After all, if God wanted nothing to do with her, she would give her attention to Satan, if that's what it took to move on.

Somebody had to love her.

The first chapter gave a history of witchcraft. It explained that while there were those who chose the path of witchcraft, there were also those who were born to it. As she read, Sarah became convinced she was one of the latter, and she wanted to learn all she could about her heritage.

Her homework forgotten, Sarah read until her father came home. They had a quick dinner together, and he left for job number two. She did the dishes and went back to her room and her reading.

Little did she know that the book which sat open before her was going to change her life.

∞

The bell rang loudly, making Sarah jump. Finally, the second period was over. She could go to third period study hall and read some more of 'Witches' Creed.'

She gathered her textbooks and notebooks, then made her way out of the classroom and into the student-filled hallway. Laughter and conversation were all around her, but Sarah kept to herself by avoiding eye contact with anyone.

She opened her locker and put her books inside, then fished out 'Witches' Creed' and locked it back up. She wanted to use the restroom before study hall, so she worked her way through the milling crowd of students and went to the girls' room.

Three girls were standing at the sinks smoking and talking. When Sarah entered, the three stopped talking and looked at her. She went into a stall, and as she relieved herself, she heard them begin to whisper, then laugh out loud at some unknown joke. When she was finished, she went to wash her hands, and she put the book face down on the small shelf under the mirror.

"So, why do you have to be so strange, Sarah?" She turned to her left to see a student she didn't know, probably a senior, looking right at her and smiling.

She ignored the girl and rinsed the soap off her hands, then grabbed a paper towel from the dispenser.

"Did you hear me?" The girl's voice had a slight edge to it. "You think you're too good to give me the time of day? Just like you were too good to spend any time with your mother before she died. Or was it that she knew you are strange and didn't want you anywhere near her."

Sarah grabbed the book and tucked it under her arm and started to leave the bathroom, but the girl caught up to her and grabbed her by the arm. "I'm talking to you, you goofy little brat!"

Sarah turned around with fire in her eyes. The three were right up to her by then, and the first one, the one that had talked to her, gave her a shove. She stumbled a bit and fell against another girl, who shoved her once again. Soon they were playing hot potato with her body and jabbing her with punches.

The girl who had been doing all the talking grabbed a handful of her hair next and flung her to the hard tiled floor. Sarah's head bounced when it struck the surface, and it was enough impact to make her see stars. Sarah's hand immediately went to the back of her head, and she felt warm blood dripping through her hair.

The restroom door opened suddenly. "What the heck is going on in here?" Sarah opened her eyes just enough to make out Mrs. Blake, the girls' physical education teacher. The woman knelt down next to her to help, and when she saw the blood she hissed, "All of you are to go directly to the main office and wait for me there. I'm going to see to it that you are all expelled."

The girls each mumbled 'Yes, ma'am," then left the

restroom silently in single file.

"My God, Sarah," Mrs. Blake said as she helped her up. "We have to get you to the nurse right away." Sarah didn't argue; her head was spinning, and her vision was blurry. If Mrs. Blake hadn't had a firm hold on her, she certainly wouldn't have been able to walk.

Soon, Sarah found herself in Nurse Moran's car holding an ice pack to the bloody goose egg on the back of her head. The nurse was taking her to Mercy General Hospital's emergency room, confident that the girl not only had a concussion but also needed a few stitches. As she drove, she spoke angrily.

"I cannot believe this happened," Nurse Moran said. "I hope you will press assault charges on that group of… of hussies!"

Sarah offered a weak smile. She didn't seem to have the energy to speak. What she really wanted was to lie down and take a nap. They were at the emergency room soon enough, and she was rushed into a room to see a doctor and receive treatment.

Six stitches later, she was told she would be staying overnight for observation. She would not be permitted to take the nap she wanted so badly, and nurses would be checking on her frequently. She lay in the bed in a double room and had the television on, but only for sound. What she was doing was reading 'Witches' Creed,' which was open wide on top of her legs.

"Oh, Sarah!" She jerked her eyes away from the book at the sound of her father's voice. "I just got the call, so I took off from work to come right away."

Kent Hathaway kissed his daughter's forehead. His face looked haggard and worn, and his eyes were filled with concern. "Who were they?"

"Who was who?" Sarah asked in return.

"The girls who did this to you. Mrs. Blake called me and told me the circumstances, but she didn't know any detail as to what started it." He sat down on the edge of her bed. "So, what started it?"

"Nothing, Dad," she said as she closed her book and set it on the tray cart next to her bed. Kent's eyes followed the book with a knit brow. "I just went into the bathroom, and they started making fun of me. I ignored them, but they started to push me around, and well, here I am."

Kent's eyes were still on the book. "What are you reading, Sarah?"

Her eyes shifted to the book, then back to her father. "Just doing some research for history, a paper I'm doing on witches in Salem. Just research."

A look of relief came over her father's face, and he looked at his daughter. Sarah continued. "So, I assume you are going to press charges on these kids? Mrs. Blake said they would be expelled, but she believes you should involve the police."

"That'll just make it worse, Dad."

Kent shook his head. "Well, it would certainly make an example out of them for other students, and it would send the message that you aren't going to be pushed around."

Sarah rolled her eyes and said nothing in response.

Kent watched her face for a moment, but it was soon obvious to him she didn't want to talk about police or charges at all. She had her face turned to the window and stared out at the sky. Finally, she broke the deafening silence in the room.

"I'm sure you know that I have to stay here overnight," she said as she turned back to her father, "You don't need to worry, Dad. I'll be home after work tomorrow."

Kent nodded and leaned forward to embrace his daughter. "I guess, I'll get myself back to work then." He stood and went to the door, opening it, then he turned back. "Sarah, if you ever just want to… talk, you know I'm here for you."

"Thanks Dad," she replied, "I love you."

Once he was gone, she looked over at the empty bed across the room. Sarah was grateful she was alone. She wanted time to read in peace. She reached for the book and opened it up once again, but this time she opened it to the appendix and began to scan the columns with her finger. No, she didn't want to press charges on the girls from the restroom. She thought she had a much better solution, one that would be much more effective in teaching them a lesson.

CHAPTER 8

The Paradise Public Library was so tranquil, she could almost hear the dust landing. Sarah stood in between two massive cases of books, but her attention was only on a single shelf of one case. She was pulling books from it, one at a time, then flipping through them to see if any contained the information she was looking for.

Sarah already had two books chosen; they were placed at her feet so she could continue to look without hindrance. She found a third book that interested her greatly, then she bent over and picked up the others and walked to a table outside of the stacks and sat down with her finds.

She was going to do it, and she hoped it worked. She was going to cast her first spell, and it was going to be aimed at those that attacked her in the bathroom. The first book contained a spell that would cause one's enemies' hair to fall out. The second offered her a spell that would make them break out in boils on their faces, and the third book held a spell that would break them out in warts all over their bodies. Sarah would cast the third spell first.

She checked the books out and headed to Wonder Mart for her shift. When she got home that night, she would get right to work on it. The spell called for a number of things, but there was not one ingredient she couldn't get her hands on. She needed mucus, mud, dry dirt, and frog slime. The latter would be the most difficult, but she already had an idea: she would walk by the creek on the way home after work. Frogs were abundant by the creek, so she was confident.

Her shift passed quickly, and before she knew it, she was walking along the creek with her flashlight. She could hear the frogs belting out their songs all around her. The darkness made it hard to narrow anything down, but after twenty minutes, she found what she came for: a frog seated on a fallen tree that was half-in and half-out of the water. He was big and round-bellied, and Sarah caught the little fella easily enough. She tucked him in the front zipper compartment of her backpack and made her way home.

"Daddy?" Sarah entered the house, gingerly carrying the bag. "I'm home!"

"In here, Sarah," came the response. "I have to get back to work. Glad I'm getting to see you."

She smiled at him as she walked into the dining room. "Let me just run my bag up. I'll be right back."

Once in her room, she pulled a small aquarium out of her closet that had housed a couple of chameleons when she was nine. Then, she put the frog inside and closed the lid before heading down to eat.

"How was your day?" Sarah asked her father as she

put a hamburger patty on a bun.

"Good," he replied, "But it's far from over, as you know."

She nodded and took a large bite out of her burger. "How does your head feel today?"

Sarah swallowed her food. "I've had a small headache, but nothing I can't deal with. I'm a good healer; the worst of it is over."

Together, they ate and talked about Kent's day job and Sarah's job at Wonder Mart. He asked how school was going aside from the assault, and she told him a joke her history teacher had told in class. The conversation was obligatory and perfunctory, like every day, but she was just thankful she still had her father to talk to.

Kent left immediately after supper, and Sarah busied herself with cleaning the kitchen. Afterward, she locked the front door and checked the lock on the back door. She made sure no windows were open, and that all the drapes were closed as well. It was time to cast her spell, and she didn't want to worry that the neighbors might see her.

Sarah got the biggest mixing bowl she could find out of the cupboard. She then fetched the frog from her room. "It says I need a lot of frog slime," she said to herself. She wondered what 'a lot' was, so she just got all she could from the little fellow and put it in the bowl. Next, she stirred as she added the dry dirt, and mud. Now the spell called for mucus; she put her own face over the bowl and blew her nose into it as she continued to stir with her left hand.

Next, she covered the mixture with a large paper towel. She put a pot of water on high to boil. When the water was finished, she slowly added it to the potion as she chanted:

"You think I am ugly,
You are ugly inside.
Hurting all others with,
Your foolish pride.
Now you will see,
That I will win.
Now the world will see upon your face,
The ugliness you carry within."

When she was finished, she wondered how she would find out if it worked or not. The girls had all been expelled, and she didn't know any of them well enough to know where they lived. She decided she would spy on them via their social media account; it was perfect.

When Sarah went to bed that night, she slept better than she had in a long time. She couldn't wait to see the results of her first spell, but mostly, she couldn't wait to see those girls suffer. She fell asleep with a satisfied smile on her face.

∞

"Can you tell me where the science lab is?" The boy's voice distracted Sarah from the contents of her locker. She closed the door to find a very good looking young man of her age standing there looking sheepish.

"On the third floor at the far end of the corridor," Sarah replied, "You're new here?"

"Thanks. Yeah, it's my first day," he said, "I'm Ryan. Ryan Morris."

Sarah smiled and held out her hand. "I'm Sarah Hathaway. My next class is on the third floor, too. If you want, we can walk up together."

"That would be great," Ryan said as he breathed a sigh of relief.

She escorted him up to the science lab and then went to Creative Writing. She found herself thinking about him briefly when class began; he was a cutie, with brown hair, brown eyes, and a perfect nose. She had to push him from her mind just to concentrate on the writing assignment for the day.

Three days had passed since she cast the wart spell. She had checked the results by stalking the social accounts of her attackers, and as of yet it seemed that nothing had happened, nor was it going to. She determined that she would cast the boil spell next, and she would do it that night before bed.

She was excited to try another spell. She was certain that when she got her hands on the right spell in the right book, she would be able to blossom in her witchhood. She was determined to stick it out and be persistent until that day came.

∞

That night, she cast the second spell. It called for a variety of ingredients, all of which she was able to gather. The chant was simple, but the potion itself took a good half-hour to complete. Once again she carried out the steps, and once again she waited patiently.

After four days of stalking the girls on social media, she realized that spell number two had not taken either. She felt a bit of frustration, but she was stubborn. She moved on to spell number three: the hair loss spell.

This spell would prove to involve much more than simple potion mixing and chanting. She would actually have to find a way to get her enemies to apply it to their heads. Because of the risk involved, Sarah decided she would focus on one person from the group: the apparent ringleader, the girl who had thrown her to the floor.

Melanie Biehl had been a problem student all through school, though she never had assaulted anyone the way she did Sarah. She came from a middle-class family and was an only child. This fact resulted in the girl being spoiled, mean, and bossy.

The Biehls lived on the other side of Paradise. Sarah looked in the telephone book, which listed one Biehl family: Adam and Christine. Sarah had no doubt that this was Melanie's mother and father.

After work one night, she went out of her way to pass the Biehl residence, and it was well worth it. Through a large picture window in the front, she was able to see Melanie clearly. She had the right place and the right person. Now she needed to get into the house.

∞

The next morning Sarah left the house early for school. She put sunglasses and a floppy sun hat on her head and rode her bike back to Melanie's house. She ended up hiding in a wooded area across the street and down from the house which gave her a clear view of the residence.

Sarah watched Adam Biehl leave in a dark-colored truck, and ten minutes later Christine and Melanie climbed into a minivan and left as well. Melanie's mother was likely taking her to school over in Harpersburg; it was the closest high school to Paradise, and since the girl had been expelled her parents had likely been forced to enroll her there.

She took off on her bike and headed to her own school. She didn't work that evening, so she could go straight home and make the potion. Then she would stake out the Biehl residence again in the morning. She would break in the back and add the potion to the family shampoo. She could care less what happened to the parents; she just wanted Melanie Biehl to suffer.

∞

Sarah sat in the wooded area behind the same tree the very next morning. She had woken up while it was still dark and put on dark jeans and a black hoodie. With her potion in a pocket, she walked across town with her head down; she didn't want to fuss with the bicycle today. She wanted to get into the Biehl's home, put the potion in their shampoo, and get things going in the right direction.

She didn't intend to go to school afterward. She was going to hit the public library and return the three potion books and check out some new ones. She wanted to get to know as many potions, good and bad, as she could. She needed to continue to cast and get as good at it as she could, and that would require lots of studies. It wasn't going to happen on its own.

Regardless of the fact that the first two potions seemed to fail miserably, Sarah had a very, very good feeling about the hair loss potion. Just the thought of it made her heart beat a little faster, and she found that she could hardly contain herself while she waited for results. It would take a couple of days, but she had a peaceful sense of confidence about the pending outcome.

She fully expected to see Melanie Biehl with head coverings on, and she expected it soon.

Adam Biehl was the first to leave the house, and just as they had the day before both Christine and Melanie left together. Sarah went down the block and turned left. She went up the block that ran behind the Biehl's home and cut through an alley until she found herself standing behind their house. The home was surrounded with a privacy fence, which pleased her greatly; she would be able to get in without drawing any attention.

She went through a gate in the fence and made sure the latch fastened behind her when she closed it. She walked up to the house and looked through a sliding glass door; the house was clean and very quiet.

Sarah tried the sliding door, and to her surprise, it slid open with ease. She entered the house and closed the slider behind her, then turned and got a good look at the place where Melanie Biehl lived. It was hard to imagine the evil woman living as well as she obviously did.

The dining room featured an ornately carved table with a glass top that seated six. The chairs had high backs and rollers on the feet. To her left was a bar which separated the kitchen from the dining room; it was filled with new, stainless steel appliances. It appeared to Sarah that the Biehls were a little higher than the middle class.

The front wall of the living room was a massive steepled picture window, through which she had first seen Melanie. A hallway was to the left of the living room, and there were five doors off of it that Sarah could see. One was at the very end, and it was more narrow than the others; she guessed it was a linen closet.

The first door to the right was a bedroom which had been converted into an office. The decorations were masculine, and a photo of Christine and Melanie sat framed on the desk. Sports memorabilia adorned the walls. This was obviously a space Mr. Biehl used.

The second door on the right was another bedroom. Posters of pop stars such as Kesha and Katie Perry hung on the walls. The bedspread on the single bed was purple, and the pillows were cased in fake fur. A desk with a laptop computer on it was near the window. A TV stand with a small flat screen was near the closet, and a boom box was on the bottom shelf.

Sarah opened the sliding doors of the closet. It was filled with all the latest fashion, and the floor was covered with various pairs of shoes. On the other side of the closet door was a vanity which held all kinds of makeup, nail polishes, and grooming items such as a blow dryer and flat iron.

She dug in the pocket of her hoodie and pulled out the bottle of potion and a small, wireless camera she had purchased at Wonder Mart. Now she looked around again until her eyes settled on a row of books on a single hanging shelf over the desk; perfect.

Standing on the desk chair, Sarah planted the camera. She would be able to keep her eye on Melanie from afar, and if the potion worked, she would know it. She stepped down and observed her work. The camera was out of sight.

Now she left that room and entered the Master bedroom. It featured a queen size bed, matching armoire and dresser. Two nightstands flanked the bed, and everything was in its place.

A door was ajar at the far end of the room. Sarah entered it to find a bathroom with his and her sinks and a toilet. Another door opened to a shower/tub combination, and another door off of that opened up to another toilet and sink. She went through yet another door and found herself in the hallway once again. The bathrooms had taken her in a full circle.

She went back to the shower and opened the frosted glass door. A bottle of Crew men's shampoo and a bar of brown soap that smelled like aftershave sat on one shelf. In the shower caddy, which hung from the shower head, was a bottle of Panta Two in One. That was what she was looking for.

She opened the bottle and poured the entire potion solution into it. Then she went into the second bathroom and found a single toothbrush in a ceramic holder: this would be Melanie's. She used the handle of the brush to stir the shampoo around before recapping it and putting it back in the shower caddy. She was all set.

As Sarah made her way out the sliding back door and through the gate in the fence, she smiled to herself. She could hardly wait to see the effects of the potion. She was so happy she even began to hum.

It was going to be a good day.

R.W.K. Clark

CHAPTER 9

"Do you spend a lot of time here?" Ryan Morris had seen Sarah sitting alone at a table in the library and approached her. "Wow. That sounded a lot like a cheap pick up line, didn't it?"

Sarah looked up from the book she was reading and smiled. "Yeah, it really did."

Ryan gave a sheepish smile. "Do you mind if I sit here?"

"Not at all," she replied as she began to move her things out of the way to give him room to put his things.

He sat down and put his bag on the floor next to him. "What are you reading?"

The smile faded from her face. "Oh, just doing some research for a report I have to write." She carefully closed the book, making sure her hand covered the title. She put her backpack on top of it and began to shove her notebooks and pens inside of it. "I was actually just getting ready to leave."

"Hey, don't let me run you off," Ryan said, "I didn't mean to crowd you."

Sarah smiled once again. "No, you didn't. I was

getting ready to leave anyway."

"So, do you think maybe we could hang out? Maybe grab a pizza sometime?" Ryan was grinning at her, and Sarah thought he had the most beautiful smile.

"Yeah," she said, "I don't see why not. I'll give you my number if you want."

Ryan got a paper and pen out of his pack and jotted down the digits. "I'll be in touch," he said shyly.

"Okay," she replied, "See ya later."

Sarah stopped at the desk and checked out her latest book on witchcraft, which had many points that made it seem more legit than many like it. It also contained incantations and practices that would help her mature in the craft, and she was excited to put them to use.

From the library, she returned home quickly. She had to change and go to work, and she had taken a bit too long at the library. While she put on her uniform, her mind turned back to Ryan. The conversation she had with him was the longest social interaction she had with anyone in a long time, besides her dad. Even if he never called her for a date, she hoped they could at least be friends; it would be good to have a friend again.

Before she left the house, Sarah turned on her laptop. She double-clicked the icon for the camera, and in seconds a black and white picture covered her screen. Melanie was lying on her bed on her stomach with an open textbook before her. She was jotting something in a notebook as she read. So, Melanie Biehl was a human being after all; she even did homework.

Sarah closed the laptop and grabbed her jacket

before she locked the house and made her way to Wonder Mart. She wondered how long it would take for the spell to kick in. Well, whether it took two days or two weeks didn't matter. She had plenty of back-ups to put to good use.

∞

"Sarah, I won't be home for dinner tonight," Kent Hathaway said into the receiver, "They offered me double-time, and it was just too much to pass on. Are you angry?"

Sarah had been called to the phone at Wonder Mart to speak with her father. She wasn't angry, but she was disappointed. They barely saw each other as it was, but she understood. "No, Dad. Of course not."

"Well," he replied, "if I don't see you sooner, I'll see you around lunch tomorrow, okay?"

"Sure thing. I love you." Sarah hung up the phone and went back down to finish her shift, which ended in forty-five minutes. Regardless of her dad's packed schedule and exhaustion, she was glad she would have the house to herself. She would take the time to cast a few harmless spells and get some practice in.

She finished up and clocked out, then made her way home as quickly as possible. The night was a bit chilly, and she was glad she had brought her jacket. Winter was just over the horizon; another winter of freezing her butt off just to get to school and work.

The last couple of days, Sarah had been playing with the idea of quitting school altogether and working full time. She would be able to help her father out more financially, and she could devote more time to the craft that seemed to preoccupy her thoughts more and more.

She was three blocks from home when she felt a car pull up beside her. She ignored it, hoping that it would go away, but to no avail. She heard the passenger window go down.

"Sarah? Do you want a ride?" It was Miriam Bailey, the pastor's wife.

Sarah stopped and turned to see the woman smiling in full at her. She returned the grin and said, "No thank you, Mrs. Bailey. I'm almost there, and I'm enjoying the fresh air."

"Are you sure?"

"I'm sure, but thanks again." With that Sarah turned away and continued on her course.

Miriam Bailey rolled the car window up and continued to watch Sarah as she walked away. She had a slight smile tugging at the corners of her mouth. She knew that Sarah had turned from the church, but that didn't matter to Miriam as much as one would think. No, she was much more interested in what the girl had turned to in its place.

∞

Sarah locked herself safely in the house and checked the other windows and doors. When she was satisfied that she was utterly alone and could not be seen, she set about getting her books and pouring over them at the kitchen table. She wanted to find a simple spell, a spell that was good and beneficial to herself.

At first, she had no idea what type of spell to cast.

She thought about a spell for friendship, with Ryan in mind, but that seemed a bit too basic to her. After all, he seemed to like her enough as it was, and she really didn't want him to like her because she made him; she wanted it to be a friendship that was legitimate. Otherwise, it just wasn't real.

Next, Sarah thought about a good health spell for her father. It would actually be a spell of protection, but her father was in excellent health. He could actually slow down for his own benefit. No, she thought, she wouldn't do a health spell tonight; she thought she could do better than that and benefit her father at the same time. She would do a spell to gain wealth for herself and Kent Hathaway.

She found a simple spell that seemed appropriate entitled 'Money.' All she would need was a square piece of green paper, nine pennies, and an envelope. She had everything she needed, so Sarah set about igniting her candles and placing them in the shape of a star on the kitchen floor.

After only a few minutes, she was sitting on the floor in the middle of the pentagram she had made out of masking tape, and she was preparing to write a dollar amount on the paper. How much did the book say to write? She realized she had left her book on the table and rose to get it when she heard a loud 'thump' from outside the large window in the dining room.

Sarah froze. She strained to hear as she stared at the window. One of the slats on the blinds was not sitting properly, and she realized that there was a two-inch gap.

Was someone watching what she was doing?

She pretended to not be concerned by grabbing the book and putting it on the floor in the middle of the diagram. Sarah then walked to the back door and opened it quietly. She stepped out into the chilly night, leaving the door ajar so it wouldn't make any noise when she closed it. She crept silently along the back of the house, and when she reached the corner, she peeked around.

There, at the window, was the figure of a person. The person looked to be about five-foot, ten inches and seemed to still be peeping through the blinds into the kitchen and dining area. Sarah could make out a backpack hanging over the person's shoulder.

"Who are you?" she said as she turned the corner aggressively, "What the heck do you think you're doing?"

The person jumped and took a couple of steps back, but in their surprise lost their footing and tumbled backward. Sarah quickly closed the gap between them with the full intent of tackling the individual and clawing their eyes out, but just as she got to them, she recognized who it was.

"Ryan!" she said in surprise. For a moment she forgot to be angry, then she thought about him peeping, and she got riled up again. "What are you doing peeking through my windows? What are you doing here?"

Ryan struggled to sit up, so Sarah reached out her hand and helped him. He stood and brushed the back of his jeans off. "I followed you home. I... I just wanted to see where you lived. Please don't be mad, Sarah. I really like you. I was just curious."

Sarah stared at him, straining to see his eyes in the darkness; she was trying to read whether or not he was telling the truth. The certainty in his voice made her think he was. None of that mattered though; she wondered how much he had seen.

"Look, I'm sorry," Ryan continued, "I wasn't trying to invade your privacy. I just wanted to see what the inside of your house looked like."

"So, you don't knock on doors like a normal person?" Sarah's voice dripped with sarcasm, but she felt her frustration with Ryan begin to fade.

Ryan shrugged, and even in the darkness, he looked sheepish. "I was afraid you would send me away. That's all, really. That's all."

"What did you see?" she asked him in a still, steady voice.

Ryan was quiet for a moment as if he were weighing his words carefully. Finally, he said, "Well, it looked like you were worshipping the devil or something." He got quiet again then said, "Were you?"

Sarah didn't respond right away; she was busy reading the look on his face. He didn't appear to be shocked or disgusted by his own suspicions, which were far worse than what she was really doing. Instead, he looked interested.

"I don't want to talk about this out here," she said as she looked around. She gave a growl and said, "Do you want to come in for a minute?"

Ryan smiled and got a bit excited. "Sure! That would be awesome!"

Sarah grabbed his hand and pulled him around the house to the back door. They went in, and she locked it securely behind them, then she went back to the dining room and adjusted the tell-tale shade. She turned back to Ryan, who was standing still staring down at the pentagram, candles, and other things she had placed inside.

"I don't 'worship the devil,' Ryan," Sarah began.

He snapped his attention back up to her. "So you're a witch then?" His eyes lit up when he said the words.

"Well, I'm a bit new to the craft," she replied. "What you see was me preparing to practice a spell, but no more."

Ryan dropped his backpack to the floor, and a nervous look came over his face. "No! Don't let me stop you! What kind of spell were you doing?"

Sarah shrugged and nervously walked toward him. "Nothing big. Just a spell for money. A little extra money would help my dad and me out greatly. He works two jobs as it is."

"Have you cast any other ones?" he asked.

"Well," Sarah said, "Three others. The first two didn't take, but I have a good feeling about the last one."

Ryan sat at the small breakfast nook next to the spot where she had made her pentagram. "What were they?"

"Can I trust you?" she asked him.

Ryan nodded eagerly. "Better than anyone. I

promise."

Sarah crossed the room and sat across from him at the nook. "Recently I got, well, beat up in the girls' restroom at school by some bullies."

"Why?"

Sarah shrugged. "No reason, really. I went to the restroom, and they were in there, and when I came out of the stall, they attacked me. Regular bully stuff, I guess, but I ended up with a bloody concussion and had to stay overnight at Mercy General."

"So you cast revenge spells on them? That's awesome!" Ryan was leaning forward in his seat, his face dancing with intrigue.

"Pretty much, but the first two didn't work," she replied, "The first one was supposed to make them break out in warts. The second, boils."

She really had his attention now. "What was the last one?"

"For the last one, I narrowed things down. I cast the spell only on the girl who gave me the concussion: Melanie Biehl," she said as she shifted her eyes away. "I don't know if it worked or not yet, but I have a feeling."

"So," he prodded, "what was the spell?"

"I made a potion that would make her hair fall out," she said quietly.

Ryan took a deep breath and sat back in his seat. "This is awesome, Sarah. But when will you know if it worked? At school next week?"

"No," she replied slowly. She was unsure how much she should share with him. After all, she hardly knew him, but he sure seemed trustworthy and genuine. "They were all expelled for the attack. After I made the potion and cast the spell, I had to put it in her shampoo, so…"

Ryan kept his eyes on her in eager excitement. When she didn't finish right away, he gestured with a waving motion for her to continue.

"I broke into her house and put it in her shampoo," she finally said. "Then I planted a mini camera in her room so I could watch her." Sarah stopped talking for only a moment, then she said, "Do you want to go look at her and see?"

Ryan jumped up fast, and she led him to her room. She sat at the desk, and he stood behind her as she pulled up the application, and in seconds they were looking at Melanie Biehl's bedroom, which was empty. In a few seconds, the door opened, and Melanie entered wearing a bathrobe, with her hair in a towel. She sat down at her vanity and turned on a blow dryer, which she began to dry her hair with.

"This has got to be the coolest thing I have heard and seen in my life," Ryan said enthusiastically.

The two continued to watch in silence as Melanie waved the blow dryer around her head. She picked up a hairbrush and began to run it through her hair as she dried it, and that was when it happened. Even on the grainy picture it was obvious.

She ran the brush through her hair once, then twice. The second time a large clump of the girl's long curly hair came out with it. Melanie looked in shock at the brush. She turned off the dryer and pulled the hair from the brush. The look on her face was sheer dismay.

Melanie ran the brush quickly through her hair again. Just as before, another long clump came out in the brush. Her mouth dropped open as she ran the brush through one more time.

Sarah had no sound with which to hear what the girl was saying, but it was obvious by the way her mouth dropped open she was screaming. It looked like she was yelling 'Mom' over and over again, and suddenly her bedroom door flew open, and her mother came rushing in.

Sarah closed the lid to her laptop as though the people she was watching could see her doing so. She stared at the top of the computer in shock for a moment. Finally, she shook her head to clear the cobwebs of surprise.

"It worked," she said. She turned to Ryan with wide eyes and a smile on her face. "It really worked."

Ryan could do no more than nod at her. Yes, it had worked. They both saw it with their own two eyes.

Neither of them spoke for several moments. Ryan was the one to break the silence.

Ryan sat down on her bed. "How does it work?"

Sarah turned to him and smiled. "Come with me, and I'll show you."

R.W.K. Clark

CHAPTER 10

Sarah and Ryan both sat in the pentagram, the candles flickering all around them. Before her were the paper, pennies and envelope. Her pen was poised in her hand.

"The book says I should cast for a reasonable amount," she said to him, "What do you think a reasonable amount is?"

Ryan shrugged. "A thousand dollars?"

Sarah thought it over. "A thousand sounds good; it's not a million, and it's not a hundred. Okay, a thousand it is."

She wrote the amount, in numerals, down on the green paper, then folded it four times per the directions for the spell. She tucked it into the envelope, then added the pennies one at a time. She placed the envelope face down in the center of the pentagram and closed her eyes.

"Prosper, multiply, grow;
Needed for care, but not for show.
I will let no other know,
It will come on the winds that blow."

Sarah picked up the envelope, licked the flap, and sealed it. She then took up the pen again and drew a bold dollar sign on it. Finally, she stood and stepped out of the pentagram.

"Okay," Sarah said to Ryan, "come with me."

She led him out the back door. On the patio right next to the door was a terra cotta planter which held small garden tools. She took a mini spade, and the two of them walked out to the largest tree in the backyard. Sarah knelt before it and dug a hole and placed the envelope in it. She covered it then and looked at the tree.

"The seeds which are planted,
Will blossom and bud with our need.
Protect what I have given over,
'Til we reap richly of this seed."

Sarah stood then, her eyes still fastened on the mighty oak before her. She was satisfied she had done it correctly. Most of all, she had a strong feeling that it would work.

"What do we do now?" Ryan asked.

Sarah smiled at him and headed for the house. "We wait."

∞

Ryan left fairly late, but he made sure Sarah had his phone number before he did. Sarah walked him to the door, and they both stood there in awkward silence for a moment. Suddenly, Ryan stepped forward and gave her a quick hug, surprising her.

"Keep me posted, okay?" he said.

Sarah nodded. "I will. On both things."

Ryan smiled at her and turned to go. He had his backpack over his shoulder and pep to his step. She watched him until the darkness swallowed him up.

Sarah locked the front door and went to the kitchen to clean up the tape from the floor and the candles. Once that was finished, she turned off all the lights on the first floor, but left on a single lamp for her father. At last, she made her way to the bedroom; she was beat, and she wanted nothing more than to hit the sack.

But sleep would not come easily. She thought about Ryan, and a nagging worry entered her heart, though she couldn't pinpoint if she were worried about him knowing what she was doing, or for some other reason. She found she liked him more than ever, especially now that she had shared such an intimate part of herself with him. It certainly didn't hurt that he was so good looking. His brown eyes were enough to drive her crazy if she looked into them long enough, of that much she was sure.

When sleep came, it was pure and restful, and Sarah dreamed of abundance and happiness. Something in her dreams told her that she was almost to the end of the dark tunnel she had been wandering through. Even in her sleep she felt relief.

She slept like a baby.

"How did you sleep last night, honey?" Kent Hathaway sat at the kitchen table looking haggard and exhausted. He had his hands wrapped around a cold cup of coffee, which he didn't have the energy to drink. Sarah knew he was fighting sleep just to spend a few minutes with her before school.

She swallowed a bite of cereal and smiled at him. "I slept like a rock, which I am hoping you will do. You know, I'm leaving in just a few minutes; why don't you go to bed, Dad?"

He looked at her with uncertainty, but finally pushed the coffee away and stood up. "I think I'm going to. You won't be mad?"

"Oh, Father! You drive me crazy! Go to bed!"

He came around the table and planted a kiss on her cheek. "I'm gonna. I work at two, but I'll be home for supper. See you then?"

"Then," she agreed.

When he was gone, she rinsed out her dishes and put them in the dishwasher. Sarah made sure the lights were out, and the appliances were off before grabbing her bag and heading for the door. She opened it to find Ryan sitting on the step.

"Oh, my God!" she said, "You scared the crap out of me, Ryan."

He stood, a smile plastered to his face. "Thought maybe you'd let me walk you to school."

His smile was contagious, and Sarah found herself smiling back. "Sure. Hang on though; the mailman is next door. I want to put the mail in the house, so my dad can read it when he gets up.

They stood together waiting. Ryan made small talk asking Sarah if she had checked her camera footage.

"As a matter of fact, I have," she replied. She was just getting ready to give him an update when the mailman started up Sarah's walk. The two stopped talking as he drew near.

"Hi, Sarah," he said smiling. He held out a stack of envelopes to her.

"Hi, Ted." She took the stack. "Thank you."

Ted nodded. "Anytime. Tell your daddy 'hi' for me, will you."

"Sure thing Ted," she replied as she started to thumb through the stack.

Ted was at the next house when Sarah said to Ryan in a panicked whisper. "Oh, my God, Ryan!"

He turned to her. "What? What's up?"

She pulled an envelope from the middle of the stack and held it up before him; when he saw it, he nearly fainted dead away.

There in her hand was a plain white envelope with a dollar sign drawn on it in pen.

"Wa…Was that our envelope?" Ryan's heart was beating fast, and he had to grab the railing on the porch to steady himself.

Sarah nodded. All she could do was stare at the piece of mail in her hand. After a moment, she got her wits about her.

"Wait here," she said.

She ran into the house and put the remainder of the mail at her father's place at the table, then she went back out to the porch. The two all but ran up the sidewalk, and when they had crossed the street they stopped. Sarah held up the envelope once again.

"Open it, Sarah."

She turned the envelope over and saw that it was still sealed. After shooting Ryan a frightened glance, she slid her finger under the right-hand corner of the flap and tore it completely open. Both of them peered inside.

There, within the confines of the envelope, was a stack of bills.

Sarah pulled the money out and fanned it to count it: six crisp one-hundred dollar bills.

"What the heck?" Sarah muttered, "Jeez, Ryan. It worked. It really worked."

Ryan could not even speak. Goosebumps had broken out all over his flesh, and he was a bit scared himself. His mouth was wide open, and his eyes were like saucers.

"It's only six-hundred," she said in a whisper. "But it's our envelope."

Ryan tore his eyes away from the envelope and looked at her. "Why do you think only six? You asked for one-thousand."

Sarah shrugged. "It said to be reasonable and realistic," she replied. "It was only my first time with that spell; maybe I'm not strong enough yet."

She dropped to her knees and opened her backpack.

She shoved the envelope deep inside, zipped it, and stood up. "Don't you tell anyone about this, Ryan. Swear."

"I swear," he replied.

The two started walking again, both silent with shock. Ryan was trying to figure out if all of it could be real. Sarah was trying to think of a reasonable explanation for the money. Did someone see her plant it? Did they dig it back up and put six-hundred in it? If they did, how the heck did Ted, the mailman, get ahold of it the very next morning, and without an address? None of it made sense; it had to be the spell.

"Ryan, I have to go back to the house," Sarah said as she stopped dead in her tracks. She began crossing the street once again.

He asked, "What about school, Sarah?"

She continued back, and after rolling his eyes in confusion, Ryan jogged to catch up to her. The two went up the side of the house and entered the backyard. Sarah retrieved the spade from the pot on the porch, and the two of them went to the big oak.

The hole where the envelope had been buried was still filled with dirt. It was the only bare spot in the grassy yard, making it easy to find. Sarah knelt and buried the spade in the ground. She dug twice as deep as she had the night before, but there was no envelope inside. She dropped the spade and sat in bewilderment.

"Well, there you have it," she said, looking up at Ryan as she spoke. "It worked."

Ryan nodded, a shocked look on his face. "It sure

did, didn't it?"

The two looked at each other with smiles on their faces. "It looks like there's nothing that can't be done." He was looking at her face as he talked, and all he could think about was how beautiful she was.

The smiles faded. They were looking into each other's eyes, and both of their hearts began to beat faster. Blood rushed into Ryan's cheeks.

"I… I… you know I really, really like you, right Sarah?" he stammered.

Now, it was her turn to blush. "I like you too, Ryan."

He leaned toward her timidly, then hesitated. Only a second passed before he forced himself to continue. As their lips touched, they both closed their eyes and reveled in the physical sensation and emotional upheaval of their first kiss.

After a moment, Ryan pulled away slowly. "I liked that, too," he said.

"So did I."

"Maybe we can do it again some time."

"I hope."

They both stood up and walked toward the front of the house. They couldn't stay back there and kiss forever; it was time to get on with their day. But Sarah couldn't deny the fact that she was thrilled. Her life certainly had taken a different turn since she started practicing the craft.

It was turning out to be the best decision she had ever made.

That evening, Ryan was lying on his bed with his hands behind his head, staring off into space. His school books were open next to him, but his lessons and homework were the furthest things from his mind. He was thinking about Sarah.

Ryan was in love, and he knew it. Just thinking about her put a smile on his face that he couldn't seem to get rid of. He said her name out loud.

"Sarah."

It sounded like some beautiful foreign language to his smitten ears. He loved the way it rolled off his tongue; he loved the way it seemed to taste like some sweet ice cream or creamy chocolate.

"Sarah."

"Um, do you think you're going to be okay, kiddo?" Kate Morris stood in the doorway grinning from ear to ear. At the sound of her voice, Ryan sat up quickly, his face instantly flushing bright red.

"Mom! You're supposed to knock you know!"

"Sorry," she said without the least bit of remorse, "I thought you were doing your homework and I didn't want to interrupt with knocking."

He growled. "What do you want?"

Kate continued to smile. "I was just bringing your laundry in. Make sure it gets put away please." She set a stack of clothing on the corner of his desk and left the room, closing the door behind her.

When she was gone, Ryan lay back down on the bed and resumed his activity of staring at the ceiling. He started smiling like an idiot once again. It didn't take him long to pick up right where he left off.

"Sarah."

∞

At the same time, Ryan was making googly-eyes at the paint job above his bed, Sarah was sitting on the sofa in the living room at her house, contemplating the soft kiss she had shared with her new friend. She was thinking about his skin and his hair, and how perfect his face looked.

She couldn't believe her luck. She was actually getting to know one of the best looking boys in the school. The best part was that he was new in town, and he had chosen her over all the other girls. She couldn't understand it, but she certainly wasn't going to question it. No, she was going to enjoy Ryan Morris for as long as she could.

She lay back against the couch and pulled the afghan from the back down over her. She started to fantasize about their next kiss. In her little fantasy, he was knocking on her door, and when she opened it he said, "I couldn't get you off my mind, Sarah. I just wanted to come and kiss you again." With that, he tangled his fingers in her hair and pulled her face to his with passion. In her fantasy, he even used his tongue.

"Sarah, what's so funny?" Kent Hathaway stood in the doorway grinning at her.

"Dad!" She sat up quickly, blushing. Thank God other people couldn't see thoughts! "I didn't even hear you come in. When did you get here?"

"Just now," he replied as he took off his coat, "I had a little extra time and thought we could eat together."

Sarah got up and headed toward him. "That would be great," she said, "What should I make?"

"Anything you want." They went into the kitchen, and Sarah opened the refrigerator. "So, who's the boy?"

Sarah flashed him a look, and Kent dropped the subject, but he couldn't help smiling to himself. A boyfriend was likely just what his daughter needed right now. He was relieved and thankful.

A half-hour later the two sat down to dinner, and the two of them talked about their day. Sarah loved to listen to her father, because it took her mind off herself. She was so happy that she still had him, and found herself cherishing the relationship they were trying so hard to build. For the first time in a long time, the two were able to laugh.

Things were improving, or so it seemed.

R.W.K. Clark

CHAPTER 11

Sarah ended up giving Ryan a hundred dollars of the money, referring to it as 'hush money.' The rest she turned over to her dad and explained it away as an early Christmas bonus. Kent didn't have the energy to question her, and he didn't want to. Even five-hundred was a lot to the two Hathaways.

She also got closer and closer to Ryan with each passing day. She tossed out the idea of quitting school because he was attending. She found she wanted to see him as much as possible, so dropping out was out of the question.

Sarah also continued to plug away at her job. She was beginning to glow a bit with fulfillment and happiness, and it seemed to her that things were better than they had been in a couple of years. She was scared to have hope, but she found herself hoping anyway.

She also monitored Melanie Biehl pretty closely. Sure enough, the girl had lost every last hair on her head. Her parents took her out of school, and she did nothing but hide in her room with bandannas tied around her head. She cried a lot, and even Sarah could tell the girl was beginning to lose weight, but Sarah didn't feel bad about it. In her opinion, the girl got what she deserved.

More importantly, Sarah practiced her spells daily. Some of them failed, some came to pass. She discovered that many of the spell books were bogus, their content was written for scamming purposes of entertainment and money-making. They produced nothing, and she determined quickly the ones that were a waste of time.

She purchased her own copy of 'Witches' Creed' online, and she also managed to buy copies of two of the spell books from the library that really worked. One, 'Casting Coven,' and the other, 'Black Manifest,' were her favorites. The spells nearly always worked, but she kept them on a small scale, just for the sake of practice.

She began to familiarize herself with the history of the craft; she was determined to learn as much as she could, and she wanted it to all be the truth. Sarah would carefully research every book she got her hands on, and this practice made it much easier to identify the bogus books from those of quality. It was important to her to hone her skills with care.

The biggest change in Sarah's life had to do with school. She didn't cast to get good grades, or even money all the time. But she did begin to fancy herself a 'superhero' of sorts.

She stopped attending school just for the lessons, and she began to pay close attention to the interactions of other students in the halls between classes. When she saw a student being pushed around or picked on, she made it a point to find out the bully's name (if she didn't already know it), and she would cast vengeance spells on the offenders. It would bring great relief to the victims, and it gave her a purpose which she felt was good.

As far as Ryan was concerned, well, he became a shining beacon in Sarah's life. They spent every free moment together that they could, and she knew without a doubt that Ryan Morris was not only her best friend, but he was also quickly becoming the love of her life, and he felt the same way. They hung out, read, watched movies, and most of all, they cast together. Ryan wasn't a direct participant, but he was her support. He helped her choose practice spells and assisted by gathering potion ingredients when she needed them.

∞

One day in January, they were walking through Holy Cross Park together. It was pretty cold out, and both of them were bundled up. The park was deserted except for them, so they took advantage of the tranquility that surrounded them. At one point, they were sitting and talking on the merry-go-round, rotating it slowly with their feet.

"I'm glad you came into my life, Ryan," Sarah said, "If only you knew how things were for me until I met you."

Until that day Sarah had been very evasive regarding life before Ryan. "So why don't you finally tell me?" he asked as he gave a couple of coughs.

"You know," she replied, "I've told you time and time again to put a scarf on if we are hanging out in the cold. Now you are getting sick."

He coughed again. "Don't change the subject. Tell me."

Sarah shrugged. "Several bad things happened, one after another," she said with trepidation, "Did you know I used to practically live at Paradise Church of Christ?"

Ryan opened his mouth, and suddenly his body was wracked with coughs. When he got them under control he said, "You?"

Sarah watched him closely. Not only was he coughing, but he was pale, and his eyes had dark circles under them. He actually looked a lot like he was the walking dead.

"Look, let's head to my house. We can warm up and have some hot chocolate, okay?"

Ryan agreed, and so Sarah took him by the hand. As they walked, she answered his question. "Yes, me. I was pretty dedicated to God then. My entire family made the church the center of our universe. Then, my grandmother died," she said, then she stopped while Ryan coughed some more. When he pulled himself together, they continued walking. "I was closer to my grandmother than anyone on Earth, and I took it real, real hard."

For the first time in a while, Sarah let herself think about Emma Holt. With the thoughts came a sharp pain in her stomach and chest, but even Sarah had to admit it wasn't as painful as it had once been; she was getting past it.

"Then, only a short time later, during church softball

season, my dog was killed," she said, "I had her most of my life, and she was in my care when she was hit and killed."

Ryan put his hand on her shoulder as they walked, caressing her. "I'm sorry, Sarah."

She shrugged. "I took that hard, too. I got really mad at God, but I got through it, thanks to my best friend at the time, Michelle Karas."

"You aren't friends with her anymore?" he asked.

Sarah gave him a half-hearted smile. "I'm sure if we saw each other we would get along fine, but she moved away for her dad's job. I wrote to her, but she never responded. I think she just… forgot me."

Now the pair walked in silence for a minute before Ryan said, "Then so soon after your dog, huh?"

She only nodded.

"I don't know what to say, Sarah," he said.

"You don't have to say anything," she replied, "You wanted to know, so I'm telling you. My grandma was bad, Mitzi was bad, and losing Michelle was bad. But those weren't the worst."

Ryan took hold of her mitten-clad hand. "Your mom?"

She turned to him. "How did you know?" She had never spoken of her mother's death; she hadn't even told him the woman had passed. When he had asked, she always side-stepped the question and changed the subject.

"I wasn't sure," he replied, "At first I assumed she left, but now, well, it's obvious."

"Yeah," Sarah said softly, "Obvious."

They turned up the walk to Sarah's house and entered the warm residence with great relief. "Make yourself comfortable," Sarah said, "I'm going to use the bathroom. I'll be right back."

Sarah bounced up the stairs and put her winter wear on the bed. She stepped into the bathroom and checked her face. Her skin was bright pink, and her eyes were watering. She thought she looked fine though, so she made her way back downstairs to make hot chocolate.

She entered the dining room to see Ryan sitting at the table. He could barely sit up straight, and he had gone from pale to white. He was hacking in coughing and seemed to be death warmed over. Sarah walked up to his chair and put the back of her hand on his forehead.

"Oh, my God, Ryan, you're burning up!"

He cleared his throat. "I don't feel so good. I think I should go home."

"You're not walking home like this," she said sternly, "Go lie down on the sofa and cover up with the afghan. I'm calling your mom. Go!"

Sarah didn't feel right about Ryan suddenly being sick. It had come out of nowhere, and it seemed to hit him like a ton of bricks. She didn't know of anyone else who was sick, so where did he get it from? All at once like that? He had been fine!

Ryan staggered from the room as Sarah dialed the number to his house. It rang twice, then Mrs. Morris' sing-song voice was in her ear.

"Hello!"

Sarah cleared her throat. "Mrs. Morris, it's Sarah."

"Sarah! Hi, honey. What's up? Ryan isn't home; I thought he was with you."

"He is with me," Sarah explained, "We went to the park, and for some reason, he started coughing. He's burning up, and he's white as a ghost. I wanted to know if you would come for him. I don't want him to walk."

Mrs. Morris took a sharp breath. "Oh! I'll be right there, Sarah. Give me ten minutes."

Sarah hung up the phone and took a peek in the living room. Ryan was balled up on the sofa with the afghan wrapped snugly around him. His entire body trembled as he shivered.

"Ryan, how do you feel?" she asked.

He groaned a bit in response, but he didn't open his eyes. Sarah knit her brow with concern and went back to the dining room.

Just then the doorbell rang. Mrs. Morris already? It had been only a couple of minutes since she hung up the phone. Who was ringing?

Sarah went to the front door and peeked out one of the windows that ran up and down the length of the door itself. Miriam Bailey stood on the porch clutching the lapels of her coat against the cold. Sarah rolled her eyes and groaned as she opened the door. Every time she encountered this woman, she felt a sense of dread. Why did she keep coming around? If Sarah or Kent wanted to talk to her or the pastor, then they would have called them. It annoyed Sarah to no end that the woman was so persistent.

"Sarah! Hi. I just wanted to stop by and say hello. I haven't seen you since that night you were walking. How are you?" Miriam bounced up and down as she tried to warm herself.

Sarah held the door open. "I'm fine. You may as well step in and warm up," she said, "I'm a bit busy right now, though and I haven't time to visit."

"Oh, well, I didn't mean to interrupt," the woman replied. Sarah noticed that Mrs. Bailey's eyes were darting over her shoulders, as if she were trying to be a bit nosy. "Is your father okay?"

"Yes, he's fine," Sarah said, struggling to keep from showing her annoyance. "I have a friend here who has suddenly taken ill, and I'm waiting for his mother to come and get him. As a matter of fact, I thought you might be her."

Just then, she heard a miserable groan from the living room. She stepped into the doorway. "Here I am, do you need anything?"

"I think I'm going to be sick…"

"Excuse me, Mrs. Bailey," she said as she ran to get a bucket from the utility closet.

She grabbed the container by the handle and sprinted back toward the living room. When she rounded the corner, she could hear Ryan heaving violently, and there was Mrs. Bailey, standing in the doorway to the living room, staring at the ill young man. Sarah took one look at her face and chills ran down her spine: Mrs. Bailey was smiling.

She saw Sarah out of the corner of her eyes and quickly took on a sober appearance. "He's very, very sick. I hope his mother hurries. Do you want me to pray for him?"

Sarah put the bucket on the floor beneath his head before she headed back to the kitchen for a cold washcloth. "No! I mean, no, thank you. I think you should be going. After all, you wouldn't want to get sick too, now would you?" Sarah was completely unable to hide her frustration and borderline contempt for this woman.

"If there is anything…" Miriam began, but Sarah ignored her and continued to the kitchen. When she returned, Miriam Bailey was gone. For a fraction of a second, she felt bad that she had been so cold and rude to her, but she quickly pushed it out of her mind. If the woman didn't like it, maybe she shouldn't come around as often as she did.

Sarah put the cold rag on Ryan's forehead. The vomiting had stopped, but his skin had taken on a gray, papery appearance. She looked down at the bucket; he had only vomited a bit into it, and the rest was on the carpet beneath. She ran back to the kitchen for hot water and towels to clean it up.

Sarah was just returning with the cleaning supplies, when Mrs. Morris rang the bell. She grabbed the knob and flung the door open. "He's in the living room, and he's getting worse."

Mrs. Morris took one look at her son, and a stricken look came over her face. "Oh, Lord. Please help me get him to the car, Sarah."

Sarah put the towels atop the vomit to cover it, and together she and Mrs. Morris tried to get Ryan to stand. His knees continued to buckle beneath him, and the two small females were unable to get him to the car. They nearly dropped him trying to get him back to the couch.

Once he was lying down again, Sarah turned to the young man's mother. "I'm calling the ambulance, Mrs. Morris. He needs to see the doctor."

"Oh, yes. Thank you so much. Please hurry!"

Sarah went into the kitchen to make the call, and Mrs. Morris held her son's motionless body, tears pouring down her face. Sarah didn't want to use the phone in the living room; Mrs. Morris was already upset, and Sarah wanted to be able to speak with the emergency operator without distraction.

With the call made, she returned to the living room. "They're on the way right now," she said.

She stood at the front window and kept watch for the ambulance. As she stood there, she got a nagging feeling in her stomach, but she couldn't quite place it. Sarah turned and looked at Ryan and his mother, and the feeling grew stronger. She knew in her soul that his taking ill was not just a case of 'catching' something. Deep inside Sarah thought that it was… intentional.

She shook her head to clear it. The ambulance came flying down Mason Avenue just then, and it swung into the driveway.

"They're here," she told Kate Morris as she hurried

to the door to let them in.

While they worked on Ryan, she let her thoughts go back to the dread she was feeling. There was something to it, of that she was sure. She was also determined to figure out what it was. She knew that something was certainly out of place.

R.W.K. Clark

CHAPTER 12

"Mrs. Morris, Ryan seems to have a very aggressive form of the flu. We have given him a saline IV for his dehydration, along with some other medications, and the other doctors and nurses are still working on him, but he has not regained consciousness."

Kate Morris listened to the physician at Mercy General Hospital with a very sober look on her face. Her eyes were still teared up, and Sarah could tell she was worried sick. She held a wadded tissue in her hand and kept her eyes fixed on the man's face.

"When can we see him?" she asked.

"Well, right now it isn't a good idea," the doctor replied, "We aren't even positive what the diagnosis is, and if it's contagious, well, let's just say your son needs you well. As soon as he either shows improvement or we pinpoint the problem, you should be able to see him. I'm sorry I can't tell you more, but we will keep you posted." He turned to Sarah. "You say this came on all of a sudden?"

Sarah nodded. "He was fine this morning. Not so much as a sniffle or anything. We walked to Holy Cross Park, and he coughed a couple of times, but nothing big. Then he broke out in a coughing fit, and we decided to head back to my house to warm up. By the time we got there, he had a terrible fever, and pretty soon he was throwing up. It was that fast."

"Hum," the doctor said as he made notes on a small pocket tablet, "Has he been around anyone who has been sick recently?"

Mrs. Morris shook her head, and Sarah told the doctor, "Not at all. He's been with me almost constantly, except when he goes home at night. I haven't heard about anyone being sick in school."

Next, Kate gave the doctor a run-down of everything he had eaten in the last twenty-four hours, then the doctor excused himself to go tend to Ryan. Sarah sat down next to Kate and gave her shoulder a pat.

"He's going to be fine," she said, "I'm sure it's just the flu like the doctor said. They'll have him up and at 'em in no time."

Sarah sat next to the grief-filled woman and watched the doctor walk away. Mrs. Morris took out her cell phone. "I have to call Ryan's father. He'll come right away from work." She began to punch numbers into the phone.

"While you do that, I am going to go out and get some air, okay?" Sarah gave the woman's shoulder a squeeze and headed for the elevator.

The air outside was brisk and almost breathtakingly cold. Sarah wrapped her coat tightly around herself and sat on a concrete bench just outside the main entrance.

She looked up at the slate-gray sky with anger.

"You'll never quit, will you," she said.

Things had been going so well, and she had nearly been over her anger at the things that had happened to her. Now here she was at Mercy General once again, this time with her boyfriend, who, it seemed, was going to be quarantined by doctors if they couldn't figure out what was wrong with him. She certainly wasn't going to ask God for help; after all, it was Him that put the boy there.

It hit Sarah suddenly, like a brick to the forehead. She would go home and find a good healing spell. She would brew whatever potion it called for and do whatever it took. She didn't have to sit around powerlessly anymore.

Sarah headed back up to let Mrs. Morris know she was going to walk home. As she took the elevator to the intensive care unit, she thought about the day's events thus far. Ryan had been perfectly fine at the beginning of the day. His color had been good, and he had been his cheerful self. He hadn't complained of any symptoms of any kind, and the coughing had started all at once while they were at the park. She supposed it was normal for whatever bug he had, but she had that same nagging feeling inside, which was very bothersome. No matter how much she tried to excuse it, she knew she was having the feeling for a reason.

She spoke with Ryan's mother, and then donned her cap and mittens and left the hospital. In ten minutes' time she was home, and she set about cleaning the rug in the living room first and foremost. When she finished, she took the stairs two at a time and shut herself in her room to go through her books.

She opened her copy of 'Black Manifest' and started to scour the spells within. She didn't want just any 'health' spell. She wanted one especially for healing. She ran her finger down the table of contents and read each and every available spell.

Finally, she came upon 'Strong Healing Spell,' and she smiled. It required many items, but all of them were easy to get. But first and foremost, the book instructed her to meditate for a time to increase her own personal strength. She did so, and by the time she was finished, she felt powerful, poised, and peaceful.

"Okay," she said as she began to gather her materials, "I need a square of white cloth." She went into the hall and plucked a white washcloth out of the linen closet. "Next, bay leaves." Easy again; she found them in the spice cabinet. She began to pile her ingredients in the middle of her bed.

"Now it calls for carnation petals." Well, it wasn't like she could find those right outside; it was January, after all. She put her coat back on and grabbed her wallet. Within twenty minutes, she was walking back in the front door of her house with a plastic-wrapped carnation from the local flower shop.

Next, she needed some mint. This, too, was in the spice cabinet, though it was the very last of it. She wrote it on the grocery list, and then returned to her room and added it to her pile.

"Sea salt," she read. She knew they had it in the kitchen, and she smiled about it. Her mother had only used sea salt while Sarah and her father preferred iodized. They used to tease her mother incessantly for it. Now Sarah looked to the sky and said, "Thank you Mom."

"Okay, a tiger's eye stone." She didn't have one herself, but she had her mother's jewelry box, and her mother had several pieces with the gorgeous translucent brown and black stones set in them. She found a ring and a pendant, both set in gold, but that wasn't what she was looking for. She shuffled a bit more, and in the smallest drawer she found it: a large chunk of raw tiger's eye that she had found while foraging for rocks when she was nine. She had given it to Amelia to have put in a piece of jewelry, but her mother refused. Now Sarah held it tightly in her hand. "Thanks again mom."

Two white candles: she already had those right there in the room. She put them on the bed. Earth. Now, this might be a bit more difficult, what, with the frozen ground. She took a tablespoon outside with a small container. She cleared the snow around the base of the house and put three tablespoons of the hard dirt in the container. On her way back to the room, she grabbed two cones of incense from the small drawer in the kitchen. Her mother always used to love the smell of it.

Almost finished.

Finally, Sarah needed holy water. This was the easiest part of all. Her upbringing in the church taught her that any member of the body of Christ could use it during prayer for healing. It was really only tap water that had been blessed, but those in the Christian faith believed strongly in its power. Sarah's family had kept a bottle of it, along with anointing oil, in the hall closet for just that purpose. Sarah opened the closet and pulled the light string. There it was, on the right, sitting there as if it had been waiting for her to come and put it to good use.

"Well, hello there," she said, "Here I am."

Back in her room she locked the door. First, she made her pentagram out of tape, then she grabbed a black marker from her desk and began. Sarah picked up the white cloth and wrote 'Ryan Morris' on it with the marker. Now she was required to draw the Eye of Horus on it, a symbol typically recognized as being Egyptian in nature. She drew it, then turned her attention back to the book.

Sarah then put the cloth on the altar in the circle. Around it she put one candle, the bottle of holy water, a cone of incense, and the dirt; these would represent the elements.

Now she would chant, and as she did, she would take a small amount of each element and place it on the cloth.

"Because of my love,
I do this.
I call the powers that have allowed me,
To be a part of them.
Air, Fire, Water, and Earth…

I beckon with reason.
The powers given to me.
By the goddesses and gods,
The powers within Ryan Morris.
Strengthen him to fight this battle.
Renew his health.
This is my own will…
So let it come to pass."

Sarah continued to chant and add the elements until her spirit told her she had done enough, just as the book instructed. She felt her spirit speaking clearly. Finally, she wrapped the leftover items in the cloth and tied its corners together, making a pouch of sorts. She held it in her hands, willing her own strength into it for the next thirty minutes.

Now she took it outside and placed it under the oak, in a spot where the moonlight could get to it. The book instructed her to do this every night until the healing was complete. Once he was well, she was to bury the pouch, along with any meaningful item of her choice, as an offering.

When she returned to the house, she thought about what she would bury with it. That was when she noticed Ryan's shoes. She removed the laces and replaced them with new ones from the junk drawer. When she buried the pouch, she would bury the laces as well.

Sarah called the hospital and asked the nurse in ICU for Mrs. Morris. According to her, there had been no change as of yet in his condition. She would stay at the hospital for the night, and her husband would relieve her in the morning. Sarah told her to keep her chin up, and that she would see her when she returned there in the morning herself.

Sarah was exhausted. The spell had sapped her of a ridiculous amount of strength, and when she went to her room and lay down on her bed, she fell asleep immediately. She dozed off with Ryan in the forefront of her mind, her love and worry keeping him there like a prisoner that would never be released. Her sleep was rocky, plagued with dreams of a faceless person who stood over Ryan's hospital bed and stared down at him, their heart filled with harmful intent.

The only thing she had any faith in, even as she slept, was the spell she had cast; it would make him well soon enough.

∞

"Sarah?" Kent Hathaway's voice came through the door. "Are you awake yet?"

"Yeah Dad," she groaned loudly. "I'll be right down."

She stood up and wrapped her robe around herself and opened the bedroom door. The smell of coffee and bacon and eggs nearly bowled her over, and her stomach began to growl loudly. When was the last time she had eaten? She couldn't remember at all, and now she was ravenous.

"Good morning, Dad," she said, "Isn't it Sunday? Are you going to church?" Her father had not been able to participate in regular church attendance due to work for months.

Kent stood up and poured a cup of black coffee. "Yep," he said, "I get to go today, alright." He was smiling from ear to ear, and Sarah found it to be contagious.

"Good, I'm glad." She poured her own cup of coffee and sat at the table next to him. "There was quite a bit of drama here yesterday, you know."

Kent sat down, a concerned look on his face. "What do you mean? What happened?"

Sarah took a sip of her coffee and ran her hand through her hair as the remnants of the prior day came pouring back into her mind. "Ryan and I took a walk, and he started coughing, just out of the blue." She took another drink. "We decided to come to the house, you know, to get in out of the cold. By the time we got here, he was burning up with fever and white as a ghost. I had him lie down while I called his mother. He started to throw up and, well, he is in ICU at Mercy. When I left yesterday, they didn't even know exactly what was wrong. If they couldn't figure it out, they were considering quarantine."

Kent searched his daughter's face, and she knew he was concerned for her over all else. "I'm sorry. Do they... do they think he will be okay? Are you feeling okay?"

"I think he will be okay," she said, "As a matter of fact, I'm sure of it. I have faith, and yes, amazingly, I am fine. That's what makes it so strange. He hasn't been around anyone who has been sick."

A broad smile covered Kent's face. "It is so good to hear you say that though, Sarah. You know, that you have faith. Do you want to come to church with me?"

"Um, I really can't. I'm supposed to be at the hospital as soon as I can get there." She did not meet her father's eyes; she didn't want him to see that she was dodging the invitation, even though she was speaking the truth about the hospital.

"Okay," Kent said, "So, I guess if we don't cross paths today, I'll see you sometime tomorrow. Oh, and I will make sure to put in a prayer request for Ryan. If anyone can fix him up the Lord can."

Sarah offered him a smile. "I love you, Daddy."

Kent stood and hugged his daughter, then he grabbed his coat and went to the garage to start the car. Sarah poured another cup of coffee and went up to get a shower. She needed to get moving.

Within a half-hour, she was clean and dressed and waiting on hold on the phone for the nurse to get either Mr. or Mrs. Morris for her. After a few minutes, the deep voice of Mr. Morris came on the line. "Hello? This is Jack Morris."

"Mr. Morris, good morning. This is Sarah. I was going to head down there, but I thought I would call and see how things are first." Sarah hoped for the best news, or any sign that her spell was working.

"Sarah, hi," he replied, "We haven't seen Ryan yet, but the nurse says they have his fever under control and he is comfortable. They say he's 'sleeping,' that he's not in a coma. He is taking both saline and his medicine through the IV."

She breathed a sigh of relief. "So he is doing better?"

"Better than yesterday, anyway," Jack Morris said.

Sarah let herself smile a bit. The good news was good news, no matter how small. "I'll be there soon then, okay?"

"See you then."

She hung up the phone and ran back to her room for her coat, hat, and mittens. It wouldn't do any good for her to get sick as well. She needed to be in her best form if she was going to be any good for Ryan.

While she was in her room, she got an idea. She had a gold chain that was pretty chunky; more for a man that a woman, actually. She got it from her box and then dug once more through her mother's jewelry box. She was looking for the Tiger's Eye pendant her mother had loved. She found it right away and looked at it with a smile. The chunk of stone was wrapped in a spiral of gold, and it was so beautiful it took her breath away. Since she had begun to practice her craft, she had learned quite a bit about crystals and stones; Tiger's Eye was a provider of protection and strength. She would put it on Ryan herself as soon as she was able to see him.

During her walk to the hospital, Sarah was lost in thought. Her mind kept going back to the day before and how quickly Ryan had been overcome by the illness. Something inside of her wasn't sitting right. Whenever she thought about his sudden coughing, fever, and vomiting, her stomach would lurch. She had never been predisposed to psychic abilities, and as a matter of fact, had never given them much credence in any case, but for some reason, her spirit told her that something was off in the situation with Ryan.

∞

Sarah arrived at the hospital a short time later and took the elevator to the ICU. The first person she saw when the doors opened was Mr. Morris. His back was to her, and he was speaking in a very animated manner to someone who she couldn't see.

She walked up the hall, straining to listen and hear what he was saying. She came up beside him and saw Pastor and Mrs. Bailey, and anger began to burn inside of her heart, though she didn't know why. All she knew was it seemed they were always popping up, and it interfered with the spells and magic she was working.

"Sarah, hello!" Miriam stood up with a broad smile on her face. She held her hands out to the girl, but Sarah took a step back.

"Hi," she replied.

Miriam dropped her hands to her sides. "It's good to see you. We just came to pray with Jack and Kate for Ryan's healing. We already have, but would you like to join us for another?"

Immediately, Sarah's mind went to the smile Mrs. Bailey had on her face while Ryan was vomiting in the living room the day before, and she felt her anger burn a little brighter. "No. You know, I think I'll pass." She made no effort to soften the edges of her tone.

Pastor Bailey's smile faltered a bit. "Are you okay,

Sarah?"

She nodded, but she didn't take her eyes off Miriam. Jack spoke up in an effort to break the tension. "Right after we hung up he woke up, Sarah. I've already seen him for a few brief minutes. They were taking his vitals and speaking with him, but I'll bet they are close to done." He touched her arm lightly to distract her from Mrs. Bailey; he could tell she was bothered. "Go ahead; they'll let you in. Room 419."

Sarah glanced at him and nodded. "Yeah, okay. I'm anxious to see him." She gave Mr. Morris a slight smile before offering a sneer to Miriam Bailey. As she walked down the corridor and watched the room numbers, she found herself feeling a bit of confusion; why did she feel such resentment and apprehension toward Miriam Bailey, a woman she had known, and at one time loved, for a majority of her life?

"Room 419," she whispered as she arrived at the door. The entire front wall of the room was glass, and the curtain was open so the nurses at the station directly across from it could keep a close eye on Ryan. Right now he was lying back on pillows, his eyes closed and his face peaceful.

"You'll need to sign the clipboard if you want to visit that patient," said a woman's voice behind her.

Sarah turned and saw a young, pleasant-faced nurse with a plump face and curly brown hair. "Oh, sure." She crossed the hall to the station and signed her name in the first empty box she could find.

"He is only allowed visitors for fifteen minutes at a

time, so please try to keep it brief," the nurse continued, "He will need his strength."

Sarah nodded and then entered Ryan's room. He turned his head almost immediately, and when he saw her, his eyes lit up. He still looked terrible, but he looked a lot better than when he was at her house.

"Hey, you," Ryan said.

Sarah smiled. "Hey, yourself." She gave him a quick kiss on the cheek and sat down in a chair next to his bed. "I don't know if I was supposed to kiss you, but I really don't care."

"Neither do I," Ryan replied in a weak voice.

"I saw the Baileys talking to your dad," Sarah said lightly as she looked around the room, "Mrs. Bailey said they had prayed with him."

Ryan nodded. "Yeah. They started in here, but I didn't want them doing it, so they went out to the waiting room."

"Are your parents particularly religious?" she asked.

Ryan gave a weak shake of the head. "No, not really. I think they just panicked about me being sick."

Sarah was tempted to tell him about her apprehension over Mrs. Bailey, but she didn't want to waste her visit on trivialities. She wanted to hear about him. "So how are you feeling?"

"Well, a little weak, a bit tired. I know I feel better than yesterday, but I'm still not one-hundred," Ryan said, "They won't let me out for two or three days, though. Not until they know I'm stable."

Suddenly, the nurse from the station poked her head

in the door. "Five more minutes, you two."

"Okay," Sarah said. She turned back to Ryan. "I have something for you." She stood and fished the gold necklace out of her coat pocket and dangled it before him. "The pendant is tiger's eye. It is a protective stone that provides strength to the wearer."

Ryan smiled. "I love it. Put it on me, will ya?"

Sarah unclasped the chain and put it around his neck. She clasped it in the front and then adjusted the enclosure, so it was at the back of his neck. Ryan held the pendant in his hand and admired it. "Thank you, Sarah," he said in a husky voice, "I'll never take it off."

"Good," she said, "I have a feeling we both need all the protection we can get." She bent over and kissed his cheek one more time. "Hurry up and get well, Ryan. Life sucks without you around, you know?"

"Ditto."

Sarah left the room and found Mr. Morris, and Mrs. Morris had joined him; the Baileys had obviously left for church. "I think I'm going to be going, you two. Call me if you need me to do anything, okay?"

Mrs. Morris stood and gave her a hug. "I'll keep you posted, honey, okay?"

Sarah nodded. "Look, Mrs. Morris, could I talk to you for a moment?"

The woman nodded, and the two of them moved down the hall, so they were out of earshot of Mr. Morris. Sarah looked at her and said, "I didn't know you were religious."

Kate Morris smiled. "We never have been, but I

think they are trying to convince us."

"Well, I was raised in their church, and I have to say, I always trusted them," she said, "But yesterday before you came when Ryan was puking, Mrs. Bailey was there. I went for a bucket for him to be sick in, and when I returned, he was heaving badly. Mrs. Bailey… well, Mrs. Bailey was standing in the foyer watching him, and she was… smiling."

A cloud passed over Kate's face and her smile faded. "Smiling?"

Sarah nodded. "I'm not saying it means anything, but it made me uncomfortable, and I tend to listen to my heart, you know?"

"Thank you, Sarah. I'll keep this in mind."

The two hugged once more, and Sarah left. She felt so much better now that Ryan had the pendant on, and she felt even better about telling Mrs. Morris about Mrs. Bailey. She knew something didn't feel right, and even though she was unsure of what it was, she wasn't about to ignore it.

CHAPTER 13

Sarah was wrapping up her Tuesday night shift at Wonder Mart, and she couldn't seem to wipe the smile from her face. Ryan would be getting out of the hospital in the morning, and she could hardly wait. The last two days of work and school without him around had been torture.

He told her he felt like himself for the first time since Saturday morning. She was relieved. She had gone home Sunday night and cast a simple protection spell over him, and combined with the pendant, she thought he was going to be fine.

Now she would be off work in a half-hour. She was supposed to have a late supper with her father, and she planned to make tacos. They were easy and delicious, not to mention the fact that they were fun. Sarah was content and happy.

She left work at six-fifteen and bounced home with her backpack on her back and her spirits high. She got home quickly and set about preparing the meal for her and her father, who would be home around seven-thirty. She turned on the radio while she cooked and sang along as she be-bopped around the kitchen.

Her pace was interrupted by the ringing of the telephone at five after seven. She answered it with a cheery, "Hello?"

"Sarah, it's Pastor Bailey. How are you this evening?"

Sarah's heart stopped in her chest. While she didn't get any bad vibes from him, she didn't want to talk to him any more than his wife. She took a deep breath and kept her tone as polite as possible.

"I'm good, Pastor," she said, "How can I help you?"

He cleared his throat, and his voice took on a serious tone. "I'm calling on behalf of the Morrises."

"What's going on?" she asked, her heart speeding up.

"It seems that Ryan has had some kind of an accident," he replied quietly.

Sarah thought her mind would explode. "What are you talking about?"

"Well," he began, "from what I understand, Ryan was taken to the laboratory for some blood tests around three. They wanted to be able to give him an 'all clear' before his discharge in the morning. The nurse who took him was taking him back to his room, and she was caught up in an emergency. According to her, she left him in his wheelchair in the corridor outside the lab, but when she got back he was gone."

"Gone?" Now Sarah's voice had an alarmed tone to it. "What do you mean, 'gone'?"

He continued. "Security and other hospital personnel began a hospital-wide search for him. After all, he had only hospital pajamas on and no shoes. They found him an hour later at the bottom of the emergency staircase between the second and third floors."

"Oh, God! I'm going down there right now," she said, her voice bordering on hysteria.

"Don't panic, Sarah," the man said, "He… he isn't conscious, and he hasn't been since they found him, but he is being cared for by the very best."

Sarah hung up the phone and stared at it as if it were a snake. What the heck had happened? Someone had to have pushed him; he certainly wouldn't have done it to himself. What about the protective pendant she had hung on his neck? Why hadn't it worked? She had read only the best books on the subject, and she was confused and astounded that it didn't work.

She turned off the burners on the stove and wrote a note for her father, who was due home for dinner. Even as she put on her coat, cap, and mittens, she felt detached and numb. Her mind was racing a million miles an hour as she tried to figure things out.

The walk to Mercy General was a blur for her. So worried was she about Ryan that she nearly got hit by a car as she crossed Easter Boulevard. The near miss did snap her back to reality, and she continued on her way a little bit more aware of her surroundings.

Sarah got off the elevator at the Intensive Care Unit, and she immediately saw the small group of people gathered by the nurses' station. Mr. and Mrs. Morris were in the company of Pastor and Mrs. Bailey once again, and immediately her skin began to crawl. She shoved the negative thoughts out of her mind and approached them quickly.

"I'm here," she said to Mrs. Morris, "What has happened? Can we talk alone?"

Kate Morris' eyes were rimmed with red as they had been for the past few days. She stepped away from her husband and the Baileys, so she could speak with Sarah in private. She dabbed at her eyes with a ragged piece of tissue and began.

"They really don't know what happened," Kate said, "Supposedly, he was taken in the wheelchair by one of the nurses to have some blood drawn and to get a chest x-ray; they wanted to be sure he was all clear before his discharge and wanted to make sure he didn't have pneumonia or anything."

Kate blew her nose and continued. "They had just finished in radiology when an emergency patient was brought by them in a panic. The nurse says she put the brakes on Ryan's wheelchair and asked him if he would be okay for a moment while she assisted with the other patient, and according to her, he told her yes. She said he was fine, even smiling.

When she returned, he was gone. She called up here, but they had not seen him. Soon they were searching the entire hospital, and finally, he was found at the bottom of the steps between floors in the fire staircase." Kate blew her nose again as new tears started to fall. "He's in a coma, Sarah! I don't know what to do!"

Sarah embraced the grief-stricken woman briefly before gently pulling away. She walked a few steps to the windows of his room. Ryan was hooked up to all kinds of machines; his face was black and blue, and he was motionless.

She returned to Kate Morris. "What happened to the necklace I gave him?"

A confused look came over her face. "Necklace?"

"Yes. I gave him a tiger's eye pendant earlier," she said, "It was for his protection and health. He is not wearing it now."

Kate looked through the glass before turning back to Sarah. "I don't know. I remember seeing it now, but I don't know what could have happened to it. I took some of his things home earlier, like his shoes and clothes, and I brought some clean ones for him to wear home. Perhaps the nurse packed it in the dirty clothes."

Kate walked up to the nurses' station. "Excuse me," she began, "Who packed Ryan Morris' things for his mother to take home earlier?"

The nurse, a plump woman, looked to her left, then pointed at a slight blond nurse about five feet away. "That was Nurse Coburn."

Sarah walked to the spot at the station where Nurse Coburn stood writing on a chart. "Nurse Coburn? I'm Sarah Hathaway; I'm Ryan Morris' girlfriend. I was told you packed his dirty clothes for his mother to take home."

The woman looked up at her with tired eyes. "Why yes, yes I did."

"Did you happen to pack a tiger's eye pendant on a gold chain? He was wearing it when I left earlier."

Sarah's foot tapped impatiently as she spoke.

Nurse Coburn got a thoughtful look on her face. "You know, I saw that necklace before he was taken down for labs and x-rays. He was wearing it. Maybe the nurse that took him would know. They wouldn't have let him wear it for his x-rays."

Sarah struggled to be patient and keep her composure. "Which nurse escorted him for tests?"

The woman shifted the pile of charts in front of her and eventually opened one that must have belonged to Ryan. She ran her finger down a sheet and then looked up at Sarah. "Kelly Smith took him. She is in the nurses' lounge on her break. Do you want me to call her?"

"Please do," Sarah said.

The woman grabbed the telephone receiver and punched a few numbers in. After a moment she said, "Is Kelly Smith still there?" She paused for a moment. "Could you please let her know she is needed at the ICU nurses' station as soon as possible?"

She hung up the phone. "She will be here momentarily, miss."

"Thank you," Sarah said. She began to pace back and forth, her mind racing. Of course, they would have taken it off during x-rays. They would not have known how important it was; they would have been none the wiser.

A petite redhead wearing scrubs with chickens all over them approached the nurses' station. She spoke to Nurse Coburn. "You paged me?"

"Yes, Kelly. This young woman here needs to talk to

you."

Sarah smiled slightly at the woman. "You took Ryan Morris for his tests earlier?"

"Yes, and I am so sorry…" she began.

Sarah cut her off. "I know you are. I wondered what happened to the tiger's eye necklace he was wearing."

The nurse's eyes immediately lit up. "Yes! He was wearing one, and they instructed him to remove it. I was going to put it with his other things, but the woman that was talking to him offered to give it to his mother. We gave it to her, and she left to come up here."

"Woman?" Sarah asked, her heart skipping a beat.

"Why yes," Kelly said, "It was that woman," she turned to point. "The one getting on the elevator now."

Sarah looked at the elevator down the hall just in time to see the Baileys before the door closed; Miriam Bailey was looking right at her and smiling.

"Thank you," she said anxiously.

She took off toward the elevator and opened the door to the fire exit, bounding down the stairs two at a time. She opened the door on the first floor to see the Pastor and Mrs. Bailey leaving through the main hospital doors. She lost no time in running to catch up.

"Mrs. Bailey!" The woman didn't turn around, so Sarah picked up her pace. Just as they got to their car, she reached them. She grabbed Miriam by her shoulder and spun her around. "Didn't you hear me calling you?"

Miriam looked stunned for a moment, then plastered her face with a smile. "Sarah! Hello. What do you need?"

"I need the necklace you took from Ryan when he had his tests," she said in a matter-of-fact tone.

Miriam's smile grew. "I gave that to Mr. Morris. He likely still has it."

Sarah looked at her for only a moment, then said, "Oh, thanks. Mrs. Morris didn't know anything about it. I'll check with him."

She didn't stand around for small talk. Sarah wanted to speak with Jack Morris right away. Five minutes later, she was getting off the elevator and approaching the couple, who were sitting in chairs in the visitors' area.

"Mr. Morris?" she said.

He turned to her right away. "Sarah, what's going on?"

"I was wondering about the necklace Ryan was wearing," she said, "The one Mrs. Bailey gave you."

A look of sheer confusion came over his face immediately. "I don't have any necklace. What necklace are you talking about?"

Sarah's heart sank. She had a feeling that was what he would say, and she was furious that she fell for Miriam Bailey's story. The woman had managed to distract her. She groaned out loud. She knew with certainty in her heart that, for some unknown reason, the woman was up to no good. She needed to figure out what and why.

"Would either of you mind if I went to your house? I need to look in Ryan's room. I have to find the necklace; it is an heirloom." The lie fell easily from her tongue.

Jack Morris stood up and fished his ring of keys from his pocket. "Not at all. I understand." He took the right key off the ring and handed it to Sarah. "Will you be coming back when you're finished? I have to work in the morning, and Mrs. Morris won't leave. I don't want her to be alone."

"Absolutely," Sarah replied as she took the house key from him, "I will be back within the hour; is that soon enough?"

He sat down next to his wife, who leaned on him with her head on his shoulder. "Of course. We'll see you soon."

∞

Sarah inserted the key into the deadbolt lock on the front door of the Morrises' dark, lifeless house. She turned it and opened the door slowly, then reached to the right and flipped the light switch, illuminating the living room. She entered the house and closed and locked the door behind her.

The only room she wanted to see was Ryan's. She had been in the Morris house countless times since meeting Ryan, and right now the place seemed dead. Usually, Mrs. Morris was puttering around and laughing, but now everything seemed cold.

Sarah went down the short corridor, and when she got to Ryan's space, she opened the door and turned on the light. His room looked like it always did: neat and tidy. His mother always kept things orderly for Ryan and his father.

She stepped inside and looked around, feeling a bit

apprehensive at first; the room seemed so different without Ryan in it. She almost felt as if she were sneaking around, but she felt compelled to figure out the mess Ryan was in. Sarah pushed the negative thoughts and feelings out of her mind and set her focus.

She had read a chapter in 'Witches' Creed' that she could not shake from her thoughts. It explained in detail about white witchcraft and black witchcraft. It talked about how enemy witches would go to insane lengths to cast spells on people that they saw as an obstacle to their own personal agenda. While it sounded insane to her, this was exactly what she expected was going on.

Sarah believed that the black witch in this case was none other than Miriam Bailey, the wife of the pastor of Paradise Church of Christ.

Even as she thought it, she believed she may be paranoid, or possibly even out of her mind. She had known Mrs. Bailey her entire life; the suspicions she had made no sense. But the more Sarah thought about the facts and the circumstances, the more convinced she became.

She turned to the closet door on her right and opened it. Ryan's clothes hung neatly from the bar on hangers; the shelf above was stacked with board games and books, and the floor was lined perfectly with shoes. She closed the door and walked over to his desk.

His laptop was closed and powered off. Ryan's backpack was leaning against the desk on the floor. She pulled out the chair and looked beneath it, but there was nothing under it. Sarah pushed the chair back in and turned to the bed.

It was made perfectly; not a wrinkle was in it. The nightstand next to the bed had a half-full glass of water and a radio alarm clock. Sarah pulled out the drawer, which held several pairs of earbuds and an mp3 player; otherwise, it was empty.

She plopped down on the bed and looked around. Everything was normal, except for the fact that Ryan was not there. Sarah had to be honest with herself: she had no idea what she was looking for, but she wasn't going to give up so easily.

She looked at the floor. Not a fragment of paper or dirt was visible on the red carpet. Right near the nightstand, sitting on the floor, was a plastic bag with hard plastic handles. The bag was marked with large blue letters: Patient Belongings. She grabbed the handles and poured the contents on the bed next to her. Jeans, a sweatshirt, and a pair of heavy socks. They were the clothes Ryan had been wearing the day he got sick at her house. Mrs. Morris had been so upset that she hadn't even washed them; she had simply left them here to be dealt with later.

Sarah noticed a white, powdery substance near the hem of the blanket. It was on the carpet and was mostly hidden by the bedspread itself. She reached down and touched it with her fingers and brought them to her nose. It had no smell that she could detect. Sarah dropped to her knees and lifted the bedspread to have a look.

Suddenly, she sucked in a sharp breath and tore the

bedspread from the bed, flinging it to the floor and sending the pillow flying. Under the bed was a pentagram; it was made out of the white powder, and it was perfect. Inside the pentagram was a wad of black cloth that was knotted at the top. Snakeskin was lying in the interior of the circle as well.

Sarah experienced fear and fury all at once. She reached for the black cloth with tentative movements, then forced herself to pick up the pace. On closer inspection it was obviously tied into knots, a flat piece of cloth formed into a small bag.

Sarah untied the cloth and exposed its contents. Nestled within were a tiny vial of blood, a massive insect which Sarah recognized as a stick bug of some sort, its body was broken in two, and a small leg bone of some animal. She sat back and took a deep breath and tried to clear her head.

Someone had cast curses on Ryan Morris.

She took the black cloth and its contents, bundled them back up, and tucked them into an inside zipper pocket in her parka. She gave the pentagram one last good look before leaving the room. The only thing on Sarah's mind at that point was getting home as soon as possible and getting her copy of 'Witches' Creed."

The weather outside was clear but very cold; Sarah's breath plumed as she walked as fast as she could toward her own home. The first thing she noticed as she approached was that her father's car was in the driveway. Hopefully, he didn't try to stop her to talk.

The front door swung open wide as she flung it

inward. She ran down the main hall, through the kitchen, and around to the staircase. Her father was sitting at the table, but he stood as soon as he saw her.

"Sarah! What's going on? Is Ryan okay?" He asked with a worried look on his face.

She sped by him and replied, "I can't talk to you right now, Dad. You're gonna have to give me a minute."

Sarah was up the stairs and in her room in a flash. She locked the door behind her and ran to her desk. There, on top of everything else, sat 'Witches' Creed.'

"Where did I read it?" she asked herself as she opened the book to the table of contents and ran her finger down the listing. For the next three minutes, Sarah flipped back and forth through the pages frantically, until suddenly she said, "Here!"

She began to read to herself.

The next four pages were filled with information on black witches. They, too, were able to cast, but they only did so in harm. Usually any harmful curses they do cast are used in one way or another to bring another witch, usually a white witch, or a good witch, under the black witch's power and authority. Curses were cast in an evil effort to gain control.

There were a variety of different spells they used, and each had a listing of ingredients or items used in the casting. Sometimes dead reptiles, other things much worse. Each item would represent the curse that was being cast. Sarah only wanted to find three ingredients: blood, stick bugs, and bones.

After only a brief moment she found all three: blood represented the curse of illness. The amount of blood one used when casting determined the severity of the symptoms. Normally the blood is taken from an animal, not the intended victim.

The stick bug represents being physically broken, as the creature itself will be killed by the black witch who cast it.

A bone was representative of death, like bones in a grave.

CHAPTER 14

Sarah sat in silence, staring at the book as she tried to process the information she had taken in. Okay, so Ryan had been cursed by a black witch. It was a three-fold curse: Ryan got sick, then Ryan's body was broken in the tumble down the stairs.

From what Sarah was piecing together the third curse would bring Ryan's death.

There was a light knock on her bedroom door. "Sarah?"

She jumped up and put the book and the black bundle under the pillow on the bed. "I'm coming."

Sarah opened the door to see her father standing there looking very haggard and concerned. "Hi, Daddy. I'm sorry; so much has been going on."

"Well, you look exhausted, and you left me a note saying something happened with Ryan." Kent crossed his arms over his chest. "So what's going on?"

"Ryan had a bad tumble down the stairs in the fire exit," she began, "Somehow he got away from a nurse, and when they finally found him, he was on a landing, all beat up. He's in a coma."

Her dad took a sharp breath. "Lord, I'll do some

praying for them while I'm at work. I have to get going; I'll give the Morrises a call when I get home and see if there is anything I can do."

Sarah took a step forward and gave him a hug and a peck on the cheek. "I think I'm going to hit the sack," she replied, "I'm worn out."

"Good girl." Kent hugged her back and after a quick wave headed downstairs. Sarah stood in her bedroom doorway listening for the sound of the front door closing and locking. When it came, she did the same with her bedroom door and took a seat on the bed to calm her breathing.

She knew; she knew in her heart who the black witch was, but the knowledge alone was blowing her away. Ever since she left the church and started heading her own way, Miriam Bailey had been acting… off.

Her outward behavior aside, her entire disposition and affect left a bad taste in her mouth. On more than one occasion, she had found herself feeling uncomfortable in the woman's presence. It had been in the way she smiled at the most inappropriate times. It was in the way she had lied to Sarah's face in the parking lot at Mercy General about the tiger's eye pendant.

But why? Why was a woman that Sarah had always known as a good Christian example and a pillar of the community tinkering with witchcraft? Why were the casted curses aimed at poor Ryan?

Sarah walked to her desk and grabbed her copy of 'Black Manifest.' She had to find out if there was anything she could do to counteract the tri-fold curse that Ryan was struggling through; the very same that could kill him. She began to pour over her books intently.

∞

Miriam Bailey sat alone in her bedroom at her vanity. She was running the brush through her hair as she did every night. As she brushed, she admired her reflection with obvious pride.

She had been a witch her entire life. She couldn't remember a time she had ever used her skills in a positive or beneficial note. Every spell and curse she had ever cast, every decision she made in her everyday life, was designed to further her along in her ultimate goal.

This was the fifth time, in all her years, that she intentionally deceived a good witch, a true good witch, to the point that they came under her dominion. It didn't bother her at all to play the long, drawn-out games she had to play with those around her; the payoff was too great. After all, it was all she lived to do, quite literally.

She would bring Sarah Hathaway to submission through heartache, as she had been doing to the good witches for years. Miriam planned it to the greatest detail.

The black spells were oh, so powerful. It had been so easy to pluck Emma Holt out of her granddaughter Sarah's life, and that was only the beginning of the game. Next came the death of her dog, Mitzi. All

Miriam did was sit in her car watching Sara walk with her dog and bounce that ball. One deft flick of her forefinger and the ball went flying. One shove of her hand through the air and the dog went after it, just in time to have its head caved in.

Next, of course, was Sarah's mother. To summon cancer that took her life so quickly, Miriam had to use a full pint of blood to perform the curse. She mixed the blood of a wart toad with it, and in no time, the woman succumbed to cancer. It had eaten her alive.

By that time, Sarah was no more than a walking open wound. She lost her love for God and the church, and she felt utterly alone. To a talented, intelligent young lady in that position, witchcraft was the ideal solution. All Miriam had to do was dangle it in her face.

Then came Ryan Morris, and Miriam became concerned. Love, in all its power, is the only thing that can distract a good witch that was being pursued by the bad. Sarah Hathaway had it bad for the boy. To put it simply, he had to go. She would use the cursed young man to make Sarah come running to her arms.

She would blackmail her with the life of someone she dearly loved. Once she surrendered, she would be sacrificed to the black gods, and in turn, they would give Miriam youth, she would cheat death, and she would remain young, at least until the next cycle.

She always chose a Pastor to marry and settle with when she chose a town to settle in; it always took away the suspicion completely from the minds of both the congregation and the local population. She could focus her energies on one girl, one who was struggling, one who was angry with her god, and she would lure her, through spells, to the craft.

Sarah was a strong one. She would be a perfect sacrifice; strong and beautiful. Once she was given over to the gods, not only would Miriam be powerful, she would live for another fifty years. That would be when the gods would require a sacrifice again.

She was patient. She would wait for the girl to come to her, which she would, Miriam knew. They always did; they always came.

R.W.K. Clark

CHAPTER 15

Sarah called the hospital and spoke with Ryan's father. She asked him if he would come to get her and take her back to the hospital. She had agreed to sit with Mrs. Morris, so he could go home and sleep. She would take the two books in her bag, and she would read them any chance she got, even if it meant going to the bathroom for privacy.

The drive to the hospital was short and sweet, though. Mr. Morris was exhausted, and it showed. He didn't throw a bunch of meaningless efforts at conversation at her, rather he asked her if she found what she was looking for in Ryan's room. She told him no, and the subject was dropped.

She found Kate Morris in an institutional-style reclining chair in Ryan's room. She had a blanket over her and her back to the door; she didn't even stir when Sarah came in. Since she was finally sleeping, she left the woman alone.

Another chair was at the opposite end of the wall, so Sarah got comfortable and took 'Black Manifest' from her bag. It was the only one she hadn't gotten all the way through, so it was a good place to start. A glance at the clock on the wall told her it was nearly eleven-fifteen; she began to read.

At first, she read nothing that even gave her the slightest inkling of what might be going on. She pressed on knowing that Ryan's very life was at stake.

By one-thirty in the morning, Sarah was seeing double, and her eyes were getting scratchy. She stood and stretched then walked out to the nurses' station. "Is there any place I can get a cup of coffee, please?"

A middle-aged nurse with lines around her eyes and pretty brown hair pointed Sarah down the hall. "Third door on the left is a visitors' lounge." She made her way there quickly.

She returned to Ryan's room fifteen minutes and two cups of coffee later. She brought a third back to the room with her and picked up where she left off in 'Black Manifest.'

Two chapters later, she was feeling very discouraged. She decided to read one more, and then she would get a couple of hours sleep before starting over in the morning. She sat forward and straight in the chair to keep from dozing off as she read.

Black Witch Rebirth

Black witches are volatile, hateful, and devious by nature. The things they apply their craft to can always be traced back to their desires. Thus the spells and curses are always harmful and damaging to others. But those who are the very worst are typically focusing all of their energies and power on their own rebirth.

The Rebirth is not pursued by every black witch.

Those who want, not only to roam the Earth for eternity, but also to control all circumstances and individuals around them, are the same who carry out a cycle of Rebirth Rituals.

The Rebirth allows for the pursuer, the black witch, to gain infinite power and youth, and it will render death powerless over that individual, for fifty-year increments. When the fifty years is ready to expire, the witch must begin the Rebirth Ritual again.

In order for this to be obtained, the black witch must either discover a good witch, or create one through by casting and luring. The black witch must then create any series of events that will spurn the white witch into submission and full surrender to them. Once full surrender is accomplished, the good witch is sacrificed to the dark gods.

Now the black witch has paid the fee for another fifty years of life.

That was it; Sarah had found it.

Miriam Bailey was a black witch, and Sarah was to be her sacrifice to the dark gods so she would live.

It hit her like a ton of bricks. All at once all of the confusion and chaos in Sarah's mind seemed to come together, and it all made perfect sense. She had been groomed for this her entire life. Miriam Bailey had chosen her and pursued her, and she then stole her loved ones and lured her in. She was going to kill Ryan to seal the deal.

She had likely been working on the plan ever since she offered her last sacrifice; her fifty years must be running out. Now all Sarah had to do was figure out if there was a way to save not only Ryan's life, but her own life as well.

CHAPTER 16

On Monday mornings the offices at the Paradise Church of Christ were pretty busy. Everyone was not only conducting regular business for the church, but they were also getting things in gear for the following Sunday. The pastor, Miriam, and the church treasurer, typically had a number of meetings all through the week, with the first one being nine o'clock Monday morning. They would go over the bills that would need to be paid that week, as well as how much the church brought in at Sunday's offering.

Several Sunday school teachers would also meet them to discuss and plan the next week's lessons. There was elementary, junior high, high school, and adult teachers. There was also the children's pastor, and he would plan the mini-sermons for the children who did not attend adult services.

The only other employee of the church who worked Mondays was the church secretary, Laura McCain. Laura was a forty-seven-year-old who had come to the Lord only five years prior. She was unmarried, had no children, and was loved greatly by the congregation. Not only that, but since she had moved to Paradise from

California five years ago, she had become part of the 'family' there; the whole town knew and loved her.

She was a soft-spoken woman who didn't like to talk about herself. She was always listening to the lives and troubles of others, and if there was anything she could do, anything at all, for anyone, Laura McCain was the first to volunteer. Any member of the church or resident of the town would bend over backward for the woman.

But there was much more to her than what met the eye. Beneath her loving and friendly face was a woman who, for nearly all of her adult life, had been a witch. She was raised in the Craft, and she walked it out every day until that fateful moment five years ago when Jesus saved her soul.

Laura had lived the life of a black witch. She had hurt and murdered and destroyed more lives to appease the dark gods than she could count or even remember. It was a burden that had become far too heavy. She turned her life over to God, and even though she would now die, having forsaken her black vows, she had never been happier in her life.

For the first three-and-a-half years she attended the church, she firmly believed she had found heaven on Earth. She lived in a small tidy house, had lots of friends, and she had a clear conscious. But about a year and a half ago all of that began to change.

The church pianist, Emma Holt, had died.

Now that, in and of itself, would not have ever gotten Laura's attention. Everybody dies, including her now. But Mrs. Holt's death reeked of evil. The woman had been a saint, but her death was smeared with a stench. Laura didn't know who, but someone had orchestrated that woman's death with the Craft. Her soul told her so.

She shook it off, and after a while, she even convinced herself that it was a bad case of old habits and beliefs dying hard. Then, after enough time passed, another church member took deathly ill: Amelia Hathaway. The night after her burial Laura dreamed that a young, teenaged girl was being chased by a faceless woman in black. She woke up screaming and sweating.

She had dreamed of the Rebirth Ritual.

At that point, Laura McCain was convinced that someone in the church was a practicing witch, and not of the good variety.

She now sat at the front desk in the main office of the church, and though she was trying to design the bulletins for the following Sunday, her mind kept wandering, and violently so. One minute she was typing on her computer keyboard, the next a picture of a girl with a slashed throat flashed before her eyes. She would type some more, then she would see in a flash a black and white dog with its head wedged under a truck tire.

Laura thought she was going mad.

At two o'clock she could take no more. She wandered out into the corridor and peeked inside the narrow windows of every room she passed. Finally, she saw the high school Sunday school teacher. Just who she was looking for.

She opened the door a bit and said, "Naomi, could I speak with you privately for a moment?"

The woman smiled and excused herself, then joined Laura in the hall. "Yes, Laura?"

"I was just wondering, it seems I heard about something happening to one of the teens in town, the one we prayed for yesterday," she began, "I can't remember his name now, but do you know what happened to him?"

Naomi nodded, and a look of pity came over her face. "Oh, yes. That boy and his family are not a member of the congregation, but his girlfriend used to be, and her father still is. He brought the prayer request yesterday as a matter of fact." She cleared her throat and continued. "He was ill with a bad case of the flu, or some other infection, and he wound up down at Mercy General. The next day he was much, much better, so the doctors planned to release him. When they took him down for final tests, I guess, he got separated from his nurse and disappeared. They searched and found him in a fire stairwell. He had a severe concussion and is now in a coma. It looked like he went down the stairs in his wheelchair."

Laura listened with a poker-face, but her heart was pounding rapidly. "You said his girlfriend used to attend; what was that girl's name?"

"You remember her, Laura," Naomi reminded her, "It was Emma Holt's granddaughter, Sarah Hathaway. Excuse me, I have to get back inside."

Laura gave the woman a smile and a nod. "Of course. Thanks Naomi."

She walked slowly back to her desk, her mind on Sarah Hathaway. Yes, she remembered the girl clearly, though they had never spoken past mutual greetings at church. She knew the girl's parents better; Amelia had volunteered much of her time at the church prior to her death, and she had spoken briefly with Kent Hathaway on several occasions before and after services.

She took a seat at her desk and continued her train of thought. If she had been a betting woman, she would have put money on it: Sarah Hathaway was the girl who had been lured, and the luring had been successful. She was no longer a member of the church, according to Naomi. Whoever the black witch was, she had managed to do such emotional and spiritual damage to the child that she turned easily to the craft. The deaths and losses the girl endured had been orchestrated, and they succeeded in their purpose.

Sarah Hathaway was a white witch, and now her boyfriend was being targeted so violently that Sarah would eventually offer herself to the black witch in his place. Then she would be sacrificed to the dark gods, and the woman who was responsible would be granted unimaginable power, and she would live, young and strong, for a number of years, moving on and beginning the entire terrible process all over again.

Who was the black witch?

She stood and took a piece of blank printer paper from the rack of the machine and sat back at her desk.

Laura picked up her pen and, giving it only a moment's thought, wrote:

Pastor Bailey,

I apologize for leaving, but I have a personal emergency that I must deal with. I will either return or be in touch as soon as I am finished. Everything is fine with me, so please do not worry.

I will definitely return at my normal time in the morning for work.

Laura McCain

With that, she put her coat on and left the building. Laura's only focus was to get in touch with Sarah Hathaway as soon as possible. If the girl had made any personal progress in the craft, she would have quite a bit more discernment than she even knew. Laura was sure if she talked to her together they could pinpoint exactly who the black witch was, and then Laura would be able to share with the girl what must be done to stop the process that had been started.

∞

Sarah had been unable to get even a wink of sleep. She stayed awake and continued to read 'Black Manifest' until the sun came up; she wasn't worried at all about missing school or work. As a matter of fact, neither of those responsibilities had even crossed her mind. All she could think about was finding out how to stop the curse on Ryan.

"Sarah, let's go down to the cafeteria and have a bit

of breakfast," Mrs. Morris was saying. The woman had woke up when Ryan's nurse came in at eight-thirty that morning, and she had done nothing but pace around the room and in the halls ever since. It was now going on eleven in the morning, and both of them were quite ravenous.

Sarah had already put her books in her bag so they would not be seen. She stood and stretched out. "That sounds good. I think I'll need a shower as well, so I'll likely run home right after that. When I get back, you can do the same, and I'll stay with Ryan."

For as hungry as both of them felt, all they did was pick at their food. Both of them had scrambled eggs, bacon, toast, and milk, but they did more staring at it and pushing it around on their plates than anything. After a while, Sarah broke the depressing silence.

"I'm going to get going. I won't be gone long, okay?" Sarah said as she reached out and squeezed the woman's hand. Once her coat was on, she grabbed her backpack and left.

The walk home took her longer than usual; she was so tired that she had basically trudged her way there. By the time, she got there it was nearly one o'clock in the afternoon. The house was still and empty, and Sarah looked forward to a bit of peace and quiet. She would shower and then take a little time to do some research on the Internet regarding what might be done about Miriam Bailey.

A half-hour later Sarah sat, clean and dressed, on the sofa with her laptop open. She sat down at a quarter of two, and by two-fifteen she was sleeping soundly, sitting straight up. Her exhaustion had gotten the best of her.

∞

Laura stopped at the Quick Mart right after leaving the church. She needed to find the name of the young man who Sarah Hathaway was dating, and she knew the story of his accident at the hospital had been printed in the Paradise Post. All she could do was hope a follow-up had been run since she didn't subscribe to the paper herself.

She purchased a copy then went to her car to thumb through it. There was nothing on the front page, and nothing on the second, but the third page had a small box article in the bottom left-hand corner that caught her eye:

Local Teen Still in Coma at Mercy General

Eagerly Laura began to read the piece.

A local Paradise teen who suffered an accident while in the care of Mercy General Hospital is reportedly still in a comatose state and in the Intensive Care Unit there.

Ryan Morris, 17, had been treated for debilitating flu-like symptoms for more than twenty-four hours. When the symptoms lessened, he was due to be released and was taken to the hospital laboratory for final testing. After the tests were concluded, reports say the young man disappeared, and a search for him ensued. He was subsequently discovered unconscious in a stairwell, and it was determined he had suffered a severe concussion.

A hospital spokesman tells the Post that Morris is still unconscious and is still being treated in the ICU. It remains undetermined what happened to the young man.

We will print updates as they are received.

Laura put the paper on the passenger seat and started her car. Ryan Morris was his name, and he was still in intensive care. That was probably exactly where Sarah Hathaway was.

She pulled her car out of the parking lot and pointed it toward the hospital, her hands tapping the wheel anxiously. As she drove, she thought about her own situation, and how this was going to affect her and the life the Lord had given her since she turned her back on the craft.

Laura knew that getting involved would be dangerous, but this wasn't about her or her safety. It was about saving the lives of two young people who had gotten involved in something they didn't understand. It was about getting the craft out of this town and away from the people of Paradise, the same people who had taken her in and loved her so much.

Yes, she had no doubt; she would see this through until the end, no matter what the end may bring.

R.W.K. Clark

CHAPTER 17

Kate Morris sat in the same chair she had slept in. She had pulled it closer to her son, and now she sat rigidly erect, holding and stroking his hand. She was grieved beyond words.

"Ryan, you need to come back to us," she said to him as tears flowed down her cheeks, "We want you well; we want to take you home."

She listened to the monitors as they kept vigil over the young man, and she rocked back and forth as she patted and stroked his lifeless hand. Kate wished Sarah was back; she felt so alone. She just needed someone there with her.

"Excuse me, Mrs. Morris?" She turned to see a young nurse standing in the door.

Kate cleared her throat and put Ryan's hand on his chest gently. She turned to the nurse. "Yes?"

"There is a woman from Paradise Church of Christ. She wondered if she might have a word with you, Mrs. Morris."

Kate ran her fingers through her tousled hair in an effort to smooth it, then she turned to a small mirror hanging over a nightstand. Satisfied, she followed the nurse out the door. She was led only a few feet away to the end of the nurses' station, where a pleasant looking woman in her mid-forties stood waiting.

"I'm Kate Morris." She held out her hand in greeting. "What can I do for you?"

The woman took hold of her hand and patted it with her other. "I'm Laura McCain; I am the church secretary at Church of Christ. How are you? How is your son?"

Kate started walking toward the visitors' area; Laura followed her automatically. They took a couple of the orange plastic chairs in the far corner, and Mrs. Morris said, "He is still in a coma. Machines and monitors… but he hasn't gotten any worse, and he is being cared for diligently. Just praying for the best."

"Well I will certainly be praying as well," Laura assured her, "I can only imagine what you are going through." She paused briefly and gave the woman a chance to process. "I came because I may have some information about Ryan's… situation."

Kate sat up rigidly, and her eyes grew wide. "What do you mean, like what happened to him in the stairwell?"

Laura wrung her hands. "Not exactly, but yes, I guess. In a way that is exactly what I mean, but before I explain, I need to make sure I'm right. I need to speak to Sarah Hathaway."

"What does this have to do with my Ryan? He had an accident; what information do you have?" Kate's voice became increasingly high-pitched as she spoke.

Laura made a gesture telling Kate to lower her voice. "I believe the things that have happened to your son in the last week were caused by... a person. I believe there is a person, locally, that has ill will for not just Ryan, but for Sarah as well. Since I cannot speak with Ryan, I need to speak with Sarah, and it needs to happen as soon as possible."

Her voice was hushed, but her point was clear to Kate; the woman didn't have time to explain, and Ryan's was in peril. At that moment, Kate Morris took Laura McCain's urgency as authentic.

"She left to go home and shower. She was supposed to come back, and I expected her within the hour," Kate thought aloud, "But that was nearly four hours ago..."

Laura jumped to her feet, an alarmed look on her face. "What is her address?" Her voice was controlled perfectly.

For a moment Kate appeared to be struggling to remember. "Three... no. Sixteen-thirty-seven Mason Avenue."

"I'll be back, Mrs. Morris." Laura dashed up the hall to the elevator and pressed the down button, but she took one look at what floor it was on and instantly changed her mind. Instead, she flung open the fire stairs and began to descend as quickly as she could.

She drove as fast as she could to Mason Avenue and found the house quite easily. A dark-colored sedan was parked in the driveway, and Laura simply pulled in behind it. Within minutes, she was ringing the doorbell and waiting anxiously for a response. She worried that the black witch, whoever she was, had already gotten her hands on Sarah.

The lock on the door clicked, and it was opened by a man whom Laura recognized as Kent Hathaway. "Hi, Mr. Hathaway! It's me, Laura, the secretary at church?"

He smiled at her. "Yes! Laura! What can I do for you?"

She looked at both the neighboring houses. "Do you think we could speak inside?"

Kent stepped aside and let Laura into the foyer, closing the door behind her. "How can I help you?"

"I'm wondering if your daughter, Sarah, is here by chance?"

"Why, yes, she is," he said as he gestured toward a door leading to a room just off the foyer.

Laura followed him into a family room, and there on the sofa, Sarah was curled up asleep. A book was closed on the floor next to the sofa, and the girl was covered up with an afghan. The curtains were closed to the light, and the girl slept like a baby.

"I need to speak to your daughter, Mr. Hathaway," Laura began, speaking in barely more than a whisper, "There is something taking place, something... evil. I am afraid your daughter has been made a target of the devil's evil schemes."

Kent's smile faded almost instantly, and a serious look came over his face. He gently took Laura by the arm and led her from the room, taking her to have a seat at the dining room table. Soon they were seated, and Kent immediately said, "Tell me everything; I knew it was something, but I cannot figure out what."

"Did Sarah go through a tragedy that made her distance herself from the church and congregation?"

Kent nodded his head. "But it wasn't any one tragedy; there were a series of painful things that occurred in Sarah's life and mine for that matter. But Sarah, well, she's a teenager. She took it hard and turned away eventually."

"What occurrences?" Laura asked gently.

Kent shrugged and his eyes watered. He wiped them with the back of his hand and continued. "First her grandmother, who she was very close to, had a stroke and died. You know, Emma Holt, the pianist.

"Next was her dog. But she actually showed signs of coming out good at the end of both, but then her mother, Amelia, was diagnosed with cancer and passed on as well. There was a definite turning point from there." Kent stopped and stood up. He grabbed two bottles of water from the refrigerator and offered one to Laura before opening his and drinking half in one gulp.

He sat back down. "But then she got attacked in the girls' room at school. She had her head split open and had to spend the night at the hospital. The girls that did it were expelled, but after that Sarah never returned to church. As a matter of fact, she has pretty much given all of the congregation the cold shoulders, especially Miriam Bailey."

Laura knit her brow. She never in a million lifetimes would have ever considered someone like Miriam Bailey would be a black witch, but that was exactly how they did it: they melded in, settled, and took their time. They cultivated a life and kept their eye out for the purest and perfect victim. They took their time, and they accomplished their goals through deception.

Miriam Bailey... Laura almost smiled.

"I must wake Sarah, Mr. Hathaway, I must speak with her."

He nodded. "Let's go then."

∞

Kate Morris had returned to Ryan's room after Laura left. She had sat down in the chair next to his bed and held his hand for another hour. When Sarah didn't return within that time, and neither did the church woman, Laura, her heart grew very concerned. She tried to call Sarah's home, but she had gotten a rapid busy signal.

All she wanted to do was go home and shower. When the hour was up, she walked out to the nurses' station. "Hi. I think I'm going to run home long enough to clean up and get something to eat. I should be back within the hour, but if there is any change, please call my cell phone anytime. My number is in Ryan's chart."

The nurse nodded politely and told her she would see her soon, then she went into Ryan's room to check on him. Kate returned as well, put her coat on, grabbed her purse, and left.

As she drove, she thought about Laura, the woman who had visited. Something was serious, and having that knowledge without really knowing the details was nearly eating her up inside. She didn't know the woman; all she knew was that in her heart of hearts she believed what the woman did say, and she felt as if she didn't send her to Sarah the consequences could be dire.

Because of that, she was satisfied to wait for answers.

Her home was dark; Jack had taken a double shift and was still at the office. He always took refuge in work when a crisis struck. It didn't bother her; there could be much worse things he could do to get his mind off the pain.

Kate made a bologna and cheese sandwich with mayo and potato salad. She ate quickly and chased it with milk, then headed to her room to get ready for a shower. That was when she noticed Ryan's bedroom door was ajar. She remembered that Sarah had been there and probably didn't close it all the way. A wave of melancholy came over Kate, and she reached into the darkness through the open door and flipped the light on.

The first thing Kate noticed was that Ryan's bed was not only unmade, but it was also torn apart. The blanket was lying on the floor next to the bed, and the pillow was at her feet near the door. She also noticed the hospital bag with Ryan's dirty clothes in it, and she fleetingly wondered why she hadn't put them in the laundry room.

"Sarah, why did you go and do this?" Kate let out a tired sigh and entered the room to make the bed. Sarah had to have done it; when she dropped the bag off the bed had been neatly made.

Kate bent down and with her left hand grabbed the bag and tossed it to the door. Then she turned to the right and took hold of the blanket. That was when she noticed the sparkling white powder on the red carpet. "What the…?"

Distractedly she threw the blanket onto the bed and got down on her knees. Kate bent over all the way to the floor and looked under the bed. Something was under there, and whatever it was it made her blood run cold.

Quickly she stood and grabbed the bed frame under the mattress. Kate gave the bed a jerk, and it rolled away from the wall easily on its casters. There, exposed in the light, was a pentagram and circle with snakeskin pieces inside.

Kate was an intelligent woman. She knew what she was looking at, and though she didn't understand it, her mind was able to easily realize and accept that something evil was happening in Paradise, and her son was involved somehow.

She ran from the room and into hers, where she grabbed the telephone receiver and began to punch in numbers. She would call the Hathaways again. That Laura woman knew this, and that was where she was supposed to have gone.

This time the rapid busy signal was gone, and the phone began to ring. It rang three times before she heard Kent Hathaway's voice. "Hello?"

"Kent, this is Kate," she began, "I tried to call you

earlier, but the line was busy or something."

"Kate! Thank God it's you!" Kent sounded extremely relieved. "The phone was off the hook, but I didn't know it until asked if I had one. I realized it had been kicked off. Listen, you need to come over here right away."

She didn't even ask why. She hung up the phone and slipped on her house shoes and coat. Within minutes, she was in the car heading to Mason Avenue as fast as she could.

R.W.K. Clark

CHAPTER 18

Miriam Bailey strode off the elevator at Mercy General Hospital's intensive care floor and made her way to the nurses' station. It was time to visit Ryan once again. It was time to get him ready for phase three.

Phase three of the tri-fold curse would mean Ryan's death, but there was one way it could be avoided: the white witch would have to take his place and turn herself, over as a sacrifice, for the final ritual. Miriam was here to complete the chant. Once it was complete, his very life hung in the balance. The outcome, whether it be death or life, would occur only after Sarah made her personal decision.

Either way, in the end, the girl would die.

She stopped at the nurses' station. A young nurse sat in a chair writing on a clipboard.

Miriam smiled at the girl. "Excuse me. I'm Miriam Bailey from Paradise Church of Christ."

The girl looked up and smiled brightly. "Yes, Mrs. Bailey! Hi! I'm Amber Johnson. You know me!"

"Amber! I didn't even recognize you in your uniform!" Miriam's smile grew; could it get any easier than this?

"Tell me, dear, is Mr. or Mrs. Morris here visiting their son? I was hoping to get some alone time with him to pray for him." Her voice gushed as she spoke.

Amber stood up with the smile plastered to her face. "Actually, no one is here visiting right now, Mrs. Bailey. You've come at the perfect time. You can only stay fifteen minutes since you are not immediate family, but go ahead and go in for a bit."

"Thank you, Amber," Miriam said, "We'll see you at the church on Wednesday, I hope."

"Yes, ma'am." The girl sat down and went back to her clipboard.

Miriam opened the door to Ryan's room and closed it quietly behind her. She turned and looked at Ryan in his bed, and she couldn't help but grin. Everything was playing out perfectly.

She walked to the side of his bed and took his right hand in her left. Her thumb stroked the back of his hand as she smiled down at him.

She remembered the look on his face when she had encountered him in the hallway after his tests. He had been so friendly and cheerful; so upbeat. He was going to be released.

She had deceived him and told him, with that smile of hers, that the nurse said she could take him back upstairs to his room. He didn't even question it. Ryan had talked to her the whole time she pushed the wheelchair.

At least, he talked until she had pushed his chair into the back stairway.

"What are we doing in here," he asked with a chuckle, but it had been a suspicious chuckle.

"We're just following through on the next step," she had told him, "It will be fast, Ryan."

"Wha…," Ryan had turned to look at her, but she was too fast for him. She raised her bag over her head, holding it by the brick inside, and she brought it down on his head hard.

"Two, two, by the power of two…
Harming you will get me through!"

She dropped the bag on the floor and shoved the chair down the stairs as hard as she could. About halfway down the flight, he had flown forward off the seat, and his head crashed into the wall at the landing. Ryan had crumbled to the floor right away, and the only noise left was the wheelchair as it crashed to the landing as well.

Miriam had straightened herself out and grabbed the bag at her feet, then calmly left the stairwell. She had smiled at a doctor as he walked by, and she had kept walking. She had even begun to hum a tune to herself.

∞

Now she stood over his peaceful body and looked at his blackened eyes and bruised chest and face. She continued to stroke his hand and gaze at his face. "It's time."

She closed her eyes only briefly, then opened them once again and, stroking his hand steadily, said.

"Three, three, by the power of three.
A sacrifice for you, an eternity for me."

Miriam repeated this, over and over, in little more than a whisper, for the next five minutes. When the surety came, it came hard to her heart, and she knew that the chant had done its magic. She coldly dropped his hand and walked over to the mirror, the broken boy in the bed forgotten.

She diligently checked her hair and makeup, then went out of the room. She passed Amber without a backward glance and made her way to the elevator, humming once again. Now she would make Sarah aware of the predicament she was really in. If the girl willingly allowed Miriam dominion over her, Ryan Morris would awaken, and he would slowly and surely get better. If she did not, he would die, and Miriam would have to cast a more persuasive curse.

Perhaps Kent Hathaway would have to play a part.

CHAPTER 19

Laura McCain sat in the living room of the Hathaway home with both Sarah and Kent. Kate Morris had just arrived, and the group was sitting discussing what was happening in Paradise. Kent, Sarah, and Kate all gave Laura their full attention as she started from the very beginning.

"Before I found the Lord I was… I was a witch," Laura began. She felt ashamed of her past, and revealing its true nature was terribly difficult, but she understood the lives that were at stake. She pressed on. "I wasn't what you would call a 'good' witch."

She took a drink of water from a glass Kent had gotten for her and continued. "As you may or may not know, I have lived in Paradise for five years, and the Lord has given me a new life. Until today, I have done everything possible to put my past behind me and go forward.

"But for over a year, actually closer to two, I have been experiencing mental pictures which flash through my mind randomly," she said, "I know this is going to be hard for you all to understand, but the pictures were warning me."

"Warning you of what?" Kate asked.

Sarah's eyes were fixed on Laura McCain's face, and Sarah said, "Of a presence. Of a bad witch."

Kent and Kate looked at Sarah in a confused fashion, but Laura looked at the girl warmly and smiled. "They began when your grandmother, Emma Holt, died."

The room was quiet as everyone waited for her to continue. "I didn't understand initially what was happening. Then Amelia, your wife, and your mother died, and it began to get stronger."

Laura reached out and took Sarah's hand. "By the time Ryan had his accident, I understood much more clearly: my spirit was sensing another black witch. Having been one myself at one time, I knew it meant only one thing. Black witches groom sacrifices, sacrifices which pay for youth and immortality, at least for a specific amount of time."

"It's me, isn't it?" Sarah was gripping Laura's hand, and her leg had begun to bounce nervously.

"You already know the answer, Sarah," Laura said quietly.

Kent leaned forward, and his voice was frustrated as he struggled to put the loose ends together in his mind. "What does this mean?"

Laura stood now and began to pace as she talked. She didn't want to leave anything out. "It means that for the last fifty years the black witch, whoever she is, has been orchestrating events in Sarah's life that would lure her to witchcraft. She would be of no use to the witch if she were not good, or 'white,' so she chose carefully and played an important part of Sarah's life since she was born.

"When Sarah became old enough and vulnerable enough, the black witch began to cast 'curses' which would cause tragedy to systematically occur in her life." She looked in Sarah's eyes. "The death of your grandmother, your dog, and your mother. Finally, the assault on you that your father told me about. It was right around that time that you turned your back on the church, wasn't it, Sarah?"

The girl nodded, her eyes growing narrow as the pieces all fell together. The black witch had literally made her entire life a lie. She waited patiently for Laura to continue.

"All of a sudden your mind turned to magic. You needed control over your life, and witchcraft would give you that without stealing who you were as a person, or so you thought."

Now Laura sat down again and continued. "The final nudge, the one that would bring all this to an end for the black witch, was the tri-fold curse on Ryan."

Kate took a sharp breath. "The star and circle under his bed," she said absently.

"Yes. It has likely been there for some time. We will have to deal with that soon," Laura said. "But the important thing, the most vital thing, is to figure out who the black witch really is and go from there if we want to save your life." She turned back to Sarah. "I think we both know who it is, don't we Sarah?"

The girl nodded as anger coursed through her veins. "Miriam Bailey," she said.

Laura did not react to the revelation, though Kate nearly passed out. "Oh, God, she's been lurking all along."

Kent put an arm around Kate to steady her. Laura continued to speak to Sarah. "You found the pentagram, didn't you? There was something... inside of it. What were the items?"

"A black knotted pouch was sitting right in the middle. It was made from a simple piece of black cloth," Sarah told her, "There were three things inside: a vial of blood, a broken stick bug, and a bone of some kind."

Laura smiled. "Very good, Sarah. The blood was the casting element for the flu that your son experienced when he first went to Mercy General. How large was the vial, Sarah?"

The girl shrugged. "About as big as one of those tubes they use when they take your blood."

"She really wanted him sick. She wanted to make sure he wound up in the hospital." She looked at Kate and Kent. "The more you use, the sicker the victim becomes. Now for the broken stick bug: that represents physical brokenness. Use of the stick bug ensured that she would be successful when she harmed him. I'm convinced she pushed the boy down the stairwell, and she likely assaulted him beforehand to make sure it went smoothly.

She would have to perform a chant over him for any

of the curses to work. The bone represents his decaying corpse; it means death. She will have to perform a chant to control the spell and set it off."

"How do we stop this, Laura?" Sarah asked in a serious voice.

Laura turned to her. "Three things can happen as a result of this curse. She will make you aware that you must submit yourself willingly to her control, if Ryan is to live. If you agree and submit, Ryan will live, the spell guarantees it.

"If you resist, Ryan will die. The spell guarantees it. You probably know that if you willingly submit she will sacrifice you to the dark gods, and she will continue to live."

Kent stood angrily. "What you're saying is that I am going to lose my daughter! What you're saying is that there is no way to win!"

Laura said, "There is only one way. Sarah must kill the black witch with her own bare hands, and it must happen without her coming under submission, or she will lose her own will and be unable."

Kent sat down and put his head in his hands. "What do we do, Laura?"

"I'm going to help her, Kent," Laura said reassuringly, "I'm going to be with her to protect and strengthen her, and she is going to kill the black witch."

Sarah looked excited. "What do we need to do first?"

Laura, Kate, and Sarah were in Laura's car heading to the Morris home. Laura made the group aware that the first thing they had to do was get rid of the circle that the black witch had cast under Ryan's bed. She had told Kent to stay home and pray, and the three women would go together. Kent had been apprehensive about Sarah's involvement, but Laura had convinced him that Sarah had to be involved with all aspects of the battle to come because it was hers. He begrudgingly agreed.

"It will be simple, Sarah," Laura was saying, "A vacuum will do. You will have to utter a white chant that will eradicate the power of the circle. Oddly enough, I remember the chant perfectly; I used to despise its power like the plague, and I feared it."

Sarah wrote it down as they drove, the dome light in the small car helping her to see. She read it over and over until she thought she had it memorized, but she tucked it safely in the pocket inside her parka just in case.

"Vacuum up the circle while chanting. Say it until you feel a release in your spirit," Laura said. She turned slightly to the girl. "You will know deep inside when it has taken hold."

She pulled the car into the Morrises' driveway, and the three of them got out of the car. As they walked up to the front door, Kate dug through her purse for her keys. "I still haven't showered. I can't believe all of this is really happening. It seems so… far-fetched." She put the key in the lock and turned to Laura. "This has to work. I can't lose my son; he's all Jack, and I have."

"I understand," Laura replied, "That's why it is imperative that we take care of things in the right order and in a timely fashion."

They walked through the front door and headed to the hallway, with Kate flipping light switches as they went. "The vacuum is in this closet," she said as she stopped and opened the closet door. She pulled it out and steered it the rest of the way down the hall to Ryan's room, where she flipped yet another light switch.

Sarah noted that the bed had been pulled out by Kate when she discovered the pentagram earlier. It would be easy to access the circle and vacuum it up in no time. She was anxious to get started.

"So what do I do first?" Sarah asked Laura.

"Well, you have the chant," she replied, "Start vacuuming and chanting, and you must continue to vacuum until your spirit breaks through and tells you it is finished. Kate and I will wait in the living room. Most all of the countermeasures we perform against the black witch will have to be carried out by you alone because you are the target."

The two older women left the room, and Sarah grabbed the vacuum right away. She plugged it in, flipped the switch, and began to chant as she plowed the machine right through the middle of the circle that had been cast.

"Demolish, destroy, for the sake of the light.
For the power of the sun murders the night.
Just as the dawn brings death to the moon.
My sun will bring death to your plans very soon."

She repeated the chant, over and over, as she ran the vacuum through the pentagram with violence. As she did her deed, sucking up the powder and the snakeskin from the red carpeting, her mind went around, and around the facts, she had learned both from the books and from Laura McCain. She continued to vacuum and chant when suddenly her breath rushed from her body and peace came over her like a warm blanket. It was finished.

She turned the vacuum off and looked at the clock on the nightstand. She had been at it for twenty minutes, but it felt more like five. She was relieved this part was over, and she began to wrap the cord around the machine before pushing it out into the hall. Laura and Kate were both standing at the end of the hall.

"You felt it?" Laura asked.

"Like the wind," Sarah replied.

"Good. Now we need to sit down and talk about the next step." The three of them went into the dining room and sat down at the table to go over what needed to happen.

CHAPTER 20

Miriam Bailey left Mercy General in particularly high spirits. She climbed into her car still humming, and she felt the warm glow of impending triumph as she pulled out of the hospital parking lot and into traffic. Yes, it was nearly time to present Sarah Hathaway with her ultimatum.

She had been working on this for the last fifty years, literally, as she had done so many times before, but this time it had been more difficult. Finding the right sacrifice evaded her for some time, but when Sarah was born, the dark gods gave her the release inside, and she knew the girl was the one. She put her long drawn out plan into action, and slowly but surely, for nearly seventeen years, she bided her time and played her cards with patience and skill.

Now the time was nearly upon her, and it always proved to be emotionally overwhelming. She would soon begin fresh, young once again, in a new town, in a new state, with new people's lives to manipulate and play games with. The truth of the matter was there was nothing more satisfying than doling out destruction for any black witch, and Miriam was not the exception to the rule.

She brought her car to a stop at a red light and continued to hum while she tapped the steering wheel to the tune. Suddenly heat came over her from head to toe, making her hair stand on end. Miriam's eyes grew wide, and a stabbing pain went from her chest to her stomach and down into her groin.

Someone had disturbed the curses she had cast; someone had broken a circle, and she knew exactly who.

The light turned green, and Miriam punched her foot down on the gas pedal hard. She had to get home quickly. Her husband, the pastor of the church, had turned a large shed in their backyard into a hobby house for her to do her crafts and other 'womanly' things in. Little did he know it was her dark refuge. She kept it locked up securely, for he could never see what was really inside or what she did in there. That was where she needed to go now. She needed to consult the darkness and find out how Sarah Hathaway broke a circle.

Miriam continued to frantically steer the car toward home, her mind racing. Sarah could not have possibly discovered how to break her circles from the books she had read. Miriam lured her only to books that would help her become what Miriam needed her to be; she had been careful not to lead her to any literature that would help her to overcome the plan. None of the books had the chants that were necessary to break a black circle.

But somehow the girl had learned what she needed

to learn.

Miriam pulled her car into the driveway and quickly got out. With her keychain in hand, she ran for the backyard, stumbling through the cold and the snow in the darkness. She reached the door and used the small penlight on her keychain to find the proper key and get it into the keyhole with no delay.

She entered her private domain and closed the door behind her. It was warm inside, so she let her coat fall from her body to the floor. Miriam then took up a disposable lighter she kept on her altar, and she proceeded to light all the candles around the circle and on the altar. Finally, she stripped her clothing from her body feverishly and dropped to the center of the pentagram on her knees.

"Oh, Dark Lords.
I have felt the pain of a circle being broken.
One of my own.
Show me, guide me.
What has taken place behind my back?
Who has led the white witch away from my snare?"

Miriam was met with silence. She swayed back and forth, her eyes tightly closed, as she waited for any response, but none came. After a few minutes, her eyes flew open, and she took up a small, sterling silver dagger in her hand.

"If you require blood.

I will give you blood!"

She slashed at her own inner forearm and immediately her blood began to drip and ooze. She let droplets of it fall on the altar and on the pentagram, then she repeated her first statement, imploring the dark gods to reveal the truth to her.

"Dark Lords, my circle has been broken!
Show me, guide me!
What has taken place behind my back?
Who has led the white witch away from my snare?"

Once again she began to sway and moan, blood dripping, eyes closed. She continued in this for nearly ten minutes; the gods would answer her now but in their time. She had given them blood; she must be patient.

When ten minutes was nearly up the voice came, low and rumbling, very nearly a growl. It sounded like several voices overlapping, all saying the same thing, all in agreement, but antagonistic to each other nonetheless.

"There is one of your own who has done this. It is one you know, yet you know her not."

Miriam's eyes flew open, and her heart began to pound. One of her own? "What does this mean? One from the false life I have made? One from the past?"

"One of your own, yet you know her not."

Miriam's hands were trembling now. "What shall I

do?"

"You must know her. You must discover her before she takes all this for herself."

The voice of the dark gods began to fade at the end of the sentence, and with it, the sense of their presence faded as well. Miriam knew it was no use to beg for more information; they would give her no more than they wanted her to have. The rest was up to her. She had to discover who was interfering, and she had to eliminate her from the equation on her own, or the last fifty years would be for nothing.

"Dear God, Miriam, what are you doing?" The voice of her husband, Matthew Bailey, shocked and surprised, broke her concentration.

Miriam did not turn around. She kept her naked back toward him and thought carefully before responding, but she knew there would be no explaining this away.

"What are you doing out here, Matt?" she asked in a quiet, but sweet, voice.

"I saw you pull in; you left the headlights to the car on," he said, "I saw you run back here. I turned the lights off and came out to see if you were okay, but clearly, you are not."

Miriam stood slowly as he continued. "How long have you been… practicing this? How long have you been one of the devils?"

"Matt, I am sorry you had to discover all of this the way you have," she replied, her back still to him, "Actually, I'm sorry you had to discover it at all, but what is done is done."

She heard him take a deep breath. "Dear Lord, in Jesus' name, I need your help," he said in a whisper. Miriam smiled when she heard it. Matt spoke up then. "Miriam, I am going to ask you to leave this home. Leave this property. I won't entertain Satan on the land the Lord has blessed me with."

His voice was serious, and she knew he meant it, but she would not, could not, do as he asked. This shed, this altar, was her lifeline, and she would not sever ties with it. Her very life depended on it.

She turned to him, her nakedness on complete display. She kept her hands behind her back, partly to distract him with her nudity, but also to conceal the dagger. "I'm sorry, Matthew, but I am unable to comply with your request."

His eyes fluttered over her body, but he forced them to look away to the floor. "You are bleeding, Miriam, and frankly I am disgusted with you. Please, leave now."

She threw her head back and began to laugh in earnest. Matt looked up at her, and a look of fear came over his face. Surely, dancing with the devil had driven his wife out of her mind.

Miriam stopped laughing as quickly as she had started. She flashed him a deadly look with her green eyes, the same green eyes Matthew Bailey had adored and stared into longingly for years. The candlelight danced off her red hair, the same red hair that had caught his attention all those years ago, the same red hair he had run his fingers through when they made love.

She bolted forward like lightning, and with a single deft thrust, buried the dagger into his chest, right in the middle, right below his rib cage. She stared into his eyes and smiled as she twisted it violently. Blood ran over her hand, and she grabbed his shoulder to steady him so he wouldn't fall.

"Come, my love," she whispered as she guided his dying body to the circle. Once inside, she removed the knife and let his body fall to the floor.

The dark gods would simply love this particular sacrifice, for he belonged to their most dreaded nemesis: The God of the Universe himself. They adored the blood of His children.

She kept her eyes fastened on Matthew as he lay dying, but she backed toward the shed door and closed it tightly. When he was dead, she cleaned herself and dressed. She had much to do.

It was time for her to speak with Sarah, and if not Sarah, she would have a long conversation with Kent. If one of her circles were broken, power would be stolen from the others. That meant the three-fold spell on Ryan had been weakened. She was furious, and she was going to make it right.

Miriam put her coat on and left the shed, locking it securely behind her. She strode across the dark backyard toward her car, purpose filling her mind and motivating her steps. It was going to prove to be a heck of a night in Paradise.

"The next step is to go to Mercy General," Laura was saying, "We need to check on Ryan, and we need to provide him with new protection, strong protection. It may not counteract the final phase fully, but it will confuse the cycle. It will buy us time."

"I had given him a tiger's eye pendant on a chain, but Miriam was able to take it from him, though I'm not sure how," Sarah said, "She even lied to my face when I confronted her. I have nothing left to use for protection."

Kate spoke up. "Tiger's eye? That stone protects?"

"Powerfully," Laura replied.

"I have a large, unset tiger's eye that I found on vacation one year," Kate said, "Could we use that somehow?"

Laura nodded. "Get it. We'll empower it with light by casting a chant, and we will wrap it in… let's see… do you have a plain white cotton handkerchief?"

Kate jumped up and ran down the hall to her room. Drawers could be heard opening and closing, and in less than a minute she returned with both items. She was smiling as she set them on the table.

"Will these do?"

Laura smiled. "Perfect! We need a candle, a white one."

"Right there." Kate pointed to a hutch behind Sarah. The girl jumped up and grabbed it and brought it to the table as well.

Laura lit the candle. "We all need to hold hands; I'll

do the chant."

"But... but I'm not a witch," Kate stammered.

"It doesn't matter. You are filled with power." Laura and Sarah both took one of Kate's hands, and the three of them closed their eyes.

The room was silent for a full minute, and finally Laura spoke.

"The power of light, the strength of sight...
All that is true and pure.
Fill this stone, reinforce its strength.
Help it overcome and cure."

She stopped and let go of the others' hands, then put the tiger's eye in the middle of the handkerchief. Laura knotted the corners together in two knots in the middle, making a small pouch. "Touch it."

All three of them put their fingers to it, then Laura said, "Dear Lord, you are the strongest of all. Bring us all through this, and protect this young man, please."

She took a deep breath and looked at Sarah, then at Kate, and smiled. "We need to go."

Five minutes later, Laura's car was being steered through the darkness as they headed for Mercy General and Ryan. "I have to tell you both something. When we were casting, I had one of my flashes," Laura said, "I can't be specific, but I am pretty sure Miriam has killed the pastor, and I think the dark gods have told her that Sarah has guidance from an outsider."

"So what does that mean?" Sarah asked.

Laura took a breath. "I don't think she knows exactly who is helping, but she is aiming to find out. That means she will want to talk to you, and it means that she will give you your ultimatum regarding Ryan."

Sarah sat back and thought for a moment. "Well, she'll have to find me first."

Laura glanced back at the girl and said, "Honey, she'll hurt anyone to get to you, so we have a lot to worry about. From here we will need to go to your home and wait; I'm positive she will go there first."

"My dad, Laura! My dad!" The girl was stricken with panic all at once.

"Call him now," she said as she pulled into a parking spot, "Tell him to leave and go somewhere safe."

They all got out of the car and headed inside Mercy General. Sarah had Kate's cell to her ear, but her home phone only rang and rang. "He's not answering, Laura!"

"Okay," she said calmly, "We will deal with this. Kate will stay here with Ryan, and we will go over there as soon as we are finished.

They rode the elevator to the intensive care floor, all of them anxious for what the next few hours would hold for them.

CHAPTER 21

Kent Hathaway knelt on the living room carpet facing the sofa. His Bible was open on the couch before him, but his hands were folded, his head was down, and his eyes were closed. He was praying feverishly to the Lord for protection, strength, and guidance for them all.

The doorbell rang, and his eyes opened. That would not be the girls; Sarah had a key so she wouldn't ring the bell. Who could it be? He finished his prayer and stood just as the bell rang again, twice this time.

Kent entered the foyer and flipped the lock. He opened the door to a smiling Miriam Bailey, and his heart froze in his chest. He knew this was not good.

"Uh, hello, Miriam," he said, forcing a fake smile, "How can I help you tonight? It's late. Are you okay?"

She clutched the lapels of her coat together and shivered. "It sure is cold out here. I can't find Matthew, and I wondered if maybe he was with you."

"No," Kent said, shaking his head, "I haven't heard from him, I'm sorry. If I do, I will tell him you are trying to find him."

He started to close the door, but Miriam put her foot in it. "Kent, my cell phone is dead. I'd like to call home again and see if he is there. Could I come in and use the phone?"

Kent looked at her, and in his soul, he knew she was lying, but what if she wasn't? He thought briefly, then said, "Let me grab my cell and bring it to you, okay?"

"Thank you," Miriam replied.

Kent turned for the living room and took his cell from the coffee table. He turned back around to see Miriam standing in the doorway of the room. She had come in anyway.

"I would like to talk to Sarah," she said in a matter-of-fact tone.

Kent shook his head. "Sarah's not here. Did you want to use this? I'm getting ready for bed, so I really can't have guests right now."

Miriam ignored him and began to pace around the room, pretending to admire the décor. "Where is she, Kent?"

He watched her warily. A heavy feeling had come into his stomach, "She's with friends."

Miriam got to the couch and looked down at the open Bible. She snickered lightly and said, "Do you have any idea how much I hate that book? It is so difficult to live my life, being who I am, and have to look at that thing, and hear it, day in and day out. But one does what one must."

She picked it up and leafed lazily through the pages, then she walked to the fireplace and tossed it in, her eyes alight with joy. The thin parchment pages began to go up in flames instantly. Kent felt anger burn his flesh.

"I want you to leave, Miriam," he said in a stony voice, "I know what you are, and I don't want you here."

She gave an evil laugh. "That's funny, Kent, considering that your daughter is the same, yet you desire her presence in your home."

"She isn't what you are, by a long shot," he replied.

Miriam began to pace again, the burning Bible out of her mind. "I stand corrected, which is exactly why I need to speak to her. You are only dragging this out by refusing me, you know."

The house phone began to ring then, and Kent immediately made a start for it. Miriam grabbed him by the arm and flashed a silver dagger before his face. "I can't let you answer that. I think you know that anyway."

He froze, his eyes glued to the knife. The flames danced off of it maliciously, and Kent sat down hard in a chair that was behind him. Miriam clucked her approval.

"That's a good boy, Kent." She turned away and took her coat off, her hand firmly grasping the dagger the whole time. "So, tell me: how much do you know about this little situation your daughter is in?"

She sat down on the couch and crossed her legs. She ran her forefinger up and down the dagger's blade, her eyes amused with it. Kent noticed the long cut on her inner forearm and grimaced.

"You're bleeding, you know," he said with disgust.

The phone stopped ringing, and Miriam looked up

at him. "Oh, that? That's nothing compared with the boo-boo Matthew suffered tonight."

Kent's heart sank. "What did you do, Miriam?"

"I did what I had to do," she said with a sneer, "I think you know what that means. It really doesn't matter. There are always casualties in a war. Now, where is Sarah?"

He looked away from her and stared at the fire. He would rather die than tell her anything. His mind was thinking about all the years he and his family had known this evil woman, all the prayers she had spoken over them. The parties, the friendships, it had all been a lie. He wanted to vomit. He closed his eyes and began to pray in a whisper.

"Stop it," she said simply, "I won't have this, not now. This is my time."

He ignored her and continued, asking the Lord to rescue them and to send this woman where she belonged. He asked Him to forgive Sarah for turning away and implored Him to use this situation to bring her back to the truth.

"Stop it now!" Her voice was filled with rage, but Kent persisted. Miriam stood and strode to him in two long steps, then reached out and slashed him across the chest with the dagger.

Kent cried out. His eyes flew open, and his hand went to his chest, and when he pulled it away, it was covered in blood.

Miriam knelt before him and looked him in the eye. Smiling she said, "The dark gods love the blood of the saints. It is like wine to them, and they love to be drunk on it. Matthew was but an appetizer to them. If I offered you, I would have brought them a meal, with Sarah as dessert. Continue to defy me, and you'll see."

She stood and began to pace again. "I cannot make you tell me where she is, but I am very patient, and I will wait."

Kent watched her walk back and forth, and his mind raced as he tried to figure out a way to kill her before she got to Sarah.

∞

Sarah, Laura, and Kate approached the nurses' station across from Ryan's room. A young blonde nurse looked up and smiled.

"Can I help you?" she asked.

Kate cleared her throat. "I'm Kate Morris, Ryan's mother. I just came back from home, and I was wondering if there were any messages for me?"

The girl turned on her swivel chair. "Let me check his chart," she said. She grabbed the large, metal-clad file and turned back to them, flipping it open. "No, no messages. One of the nurses logged here that there was one visitor. The pastor's wife from Paradise Church of Christ. She didn't log when the visitor left, but she noted here that when she checked the patient, the woman was already gone."

Kate looked at Laura anxiously, then said, "Thank you. They will come in with me for a moment to pray for him, then they will be leaving."

"That's fine, Mrs. Morris." The woman smiled and

went back to her paperwork.

The three of them entered Ryan's room and closed the door. "If Miriam was here, it was to cast a chant for the third part of the tri-fold curse," Laura said simply.

"What does that mean?" Kate asked.

Laura reached out and patted the woman consolingly on the arm. "It only means that once Sarah either submits or refuses, the final phase will take place. It only empowers the final phase when it takes place."

She walked up to Ryan's bed and looked down at him. "When Sarah broke the circle under his bed, she weakened that, however." She held the stone up. "Now, we will give him the stone of protection, and that has the power to stop this altogether, if we are successful in eliminating the black witch." Laura motioned for the other two to join her at his bedside.

All of them stood looking down on him. Kate had silent teardrops running down her cheeks, but the look on her face was determined. Laura took the white pouch with the blessed tiger's eye and laid it on the boy's chest. She then reached out for the hands of the other two.

"Surround him, enlighten him,
Heal him, restore him.
Protect him, strengthen him,
Provide for him.
Block the black from his presence.
Seal him in your warmth and love."

Laura then took the pouch and grasped his pillowcase. She buried the pouch deep inside the pillowcase. It was safe beneath his body. Then she looked at Kate. "We have just made a massive dent in the process as far as Ryan is concerned." She gave the woman a hug and turned to Sarah.

"It's time to go home, Sarah."

Kate watched as they left, then she collapsed in her chair in a flood of tears. "God, I don't know you, but please, please make this all okay."

She then took her son's hand in her own and sat back, stroking his soft flesh.

R.W.K. Clark

CHAPTER 22

"I want to see Sarah's room."

Miriam was standing before Kent, who had refused to look at her or speak to her since she cut him. He continued to pray in the confines of his mind and had begun to calm down quite a bit.

He looked up at her, shook his head, then looked away.

Miriam shrugged. "You can either come with me, or I can kill you now and go alone," she said simply.

"Just go," he replied, "You don't need me to help you carry out your schemes."

Miriam nodded. "You're right, I don't. But I do need you to dangle before your precious darling daughter. See, Kent, the end of this, that is going to come, is inevitable. It is set in stone." She grabbed him by the arm and jerked him to his feet. "Let's go see Sarah's room."

Kent resisted her all the way upstairs, making it very difficult to make progress. Twice she hit him in the head with her fist, and twice he laughed at her. By the time they were on the second floor, she had had enough of him.

"Let's go to your room instead," she said.

They crossed the threshold to Kent's room, and Miriam flipped on the light. She grabbed a chair from the vanity that had once belonged to Amelia and set it in the middle of the room. "Sit down, Kent."

He did, just to avoid more injury. Miriam rooted through his drawers until she found his ties, and she brought out a large number of them. She spent the next ten minutes tying him to the chair, and when she was done, he knew he wasn't going anywhere. She had plenty of practice binding people.

At last, she stood behind him and put a final tie in his mouth. As she tied it tightly behind his head she said, "It will be good to have you out of my hair for a while. Soon your daughter will return, and if my suspicions are correct, she'll have her little helper with her, whoever it is." She came and stood before him, admiring her work. "I'm excited to see who got their dirty little fingers in my pie."

Miriam turned and walked out of the room, closing the door behind her. Immediately, Kent began to squirm as he tried to undo his ties. He knew they all had a very long night ahead of them.

∞

Laura pulled the car out of the Mercy General parking lot and began to speed in the direction of Sarah's home.

"Oh, crap," she said, "I'm going to have to stop for gas."

She pulled into the Quick Mart and lined the car up

with the gas pumps. "Here, Sarah. Go inside and give them twenty on pump number two." She handed the girl the money, and she readily jumped out of the vehicle and headed inside the store. Laura watched her for a second and smiled before getting out to pump the gas.

By the time she returned to the car, Laura had it started and ready to go. "We have wasted a lot of time. I am anxious to get to your house. I think we both know that Miriam is there, and God only knows what she is doing, or at least trying to do."

She whipped the car out of the station and took a right. They were finally going to Sarah's, and the girl was more than relieved. It seemed they had wasted far too much time, and the concern she felt for her father was overwhelming. Miriam Bailey had gone to great lengths to accomplish her purpose, and she had so far been successful in a lot of ways. If she wanted to get her hands on Sarah, like Laura said she did, she definitely had a head start.

"I think we should stop at the Baileys' home and see if perhaps Miriam is there," Laura said as she sped down the street.

Sarah turned to the woman in a panic. "My dad didn't answer the phone, and he knows and understands all that is going on Laura! I'm worried!"

Laura kept her eyes on the road. "Any witch, black or white, will have a main altar. Do you understand what I am saying?"

"No, Laura. I don't." The nervousness Sarah felt in

her stomach had been growing by the minute, and the thought of making yet another stop nearly made her physically ill.

Laura sighed. "Some chants and spells must be cast before she can ever take possession of you, if that is what happens," she said, "She would have to be able to do them freely, from a circle and an altar that is her very own, that has tasted her own blood. It would be somewhere in her home, and if we can locate it and find her, we could stop this before it goes any further."

Sarah didn't even have to think. She was instantly convinced of the truth by Laura's knowledge and solidarity. "Okay. Whatever you believe we must do, do it."

"Good girl," Laura said with a smile. She took the next right sharply. They swerved, then the woman was able to regain control of the car. "Their home is only two blocks ahead, as you know. It will take us no time to speak to Pastor Bailey and give the property a once-over and find Miriam's altar."

In only minutes, Laura was pulling into the Baileys' driveway. There was a single light on at the rear of the house inside; Sarah knew it was a kitchen light. Otherwise, there was no sign of life whatsoever.

Laura left the vehicle running, and they got out of the car and ran up to the front door. Laura knocked while Sarah rang the doorbell, not once, but three times. They both stood, hopping in the cold, waiting for either a voice or a physical response, but none came.

"Maybe Pastor Bailey is in the kitchen, where the

light came from, perhaps he can't hear us," Sarah suggested.

They bolted from the front porch and headed for the back door. Sarah began to pound on the door while yelling for the pastor. Suddenly, Laura stopped her by touching her arm.

"Sarah…" she said.

The girl turned to her. "What?"

Laura looked at her in the darkness. "The hobby house. The shed out back, it's Miriam's hobby house. I've never been inside, but I know she keeps it locked up tight."

They wasted no time running through the backyard, both of them stumbling at least once. By the time they reached the shed and tried the door, both of them were out of breath. Laura tried the door but to no avail.

"This is it, Sarah," she said, "My spirit feels it."

They walked around the small structure trying to find a window, but there was none. Finally, Laura grabbed Sarah's arm and said, "We have to break the door down."

Back at the door, they both threw their weight against it over and over, but the door wouldn't budge. Laura walked to the side of the shed where a pile of cut firewood was piled beneath a tarp. "Help me get the biggest piece we can find," she said.

They pulled the tarp back and found a long, thick piece on the very end. Together they lifted it and carried it back to the door. With each grasping the wood, they swung it at the door near the knob and lock, striking it as hard as they could.

"Again!" Laura commanded. They swung again. This time the door actually gave a bit, and Sarah was encouraged. Without words, they swung it once, twice, a third time, the lock broke, and the door crashed in.

Both Sarah and Laura dropped the log and stepped inside. Candlelight illuminated the interior, and as soon as Sarah got a look, she drew in a sharp breath. She was in no way prepared for what she saw.

Pastor Matthew Bailey was lying dead in the very center of a pentagram. The white shirt he wore was covered in blood at the chest, and his eyes were wide open in shock; he had not expected what he had gotten. Sarah fell to her knees and reached out, closing his eyes. Tears fell from her own as she did so.

She turned to Laura. "She killed him."

"Not only did she kill him, Sarah, but she also offered his blood to the dark gods," Laura replied, "They are certainly pleased with her for this. Now I know she is at your home. We have to go… now!"

To Sarah, the distance to the idling car was far too long. Her feet seemed to be stuck in molasses rather than snow as she ran, and she felt confused and frustrated by the sensation. They finally reached the car, jumped in, and sped out of the drive.

Finally, Sarah thought. They were finally heading to her home. But just as she was reveling in the feeling of relief, Laura burst out, "Oh, no!"

Sarah turned to her. "What, Laura? What?"

"We're being pulled over!"

Sarah turned around to see a police car, lights flashing, right on their tail. "Oh, God, we just don't need this now!"

Laura slowed the vehicle and began to pull over. "We can't refuse to stop. We have to comply. Everything is going to be fine." She eased the car along the curb, put it in park, and turned the ignition off.

Sarah's leg was bouncing with anxiety. It seemed forever before the officer approached the car, and she kept turning around to try and see what was finally taking so long. At last she saw the cop, flashlight in hand, heading to the driver's window.

"Here he is," she said anxiously. She looked at Laura, who was completely calm. Sarah found herself envious of the woman's composure and self-control.

Laura rolled the window down. "Do you have any idea how fast you were going, ma'am?" The officer's tone was angry and annoyed.

"Yes, officer," Laura said sheepishly, "My friend's daughter has a personal family emergency at home, and my speed was a bit out of control."

He grunted. "Well, I need your license, registration, and proof of insurance."

Laura flipped open the console between the seats and pulled out some items. She handed them to the officer and then grabbed her purse from the floor of the back seat. She handed her license over as well and sat back against the seat.

"I'll be back," the cop said gruffly, and Laura rolled her window up.

"Try to calm down, Sarah," she said, "We have to trust that it is all going to work out. When we lose faith, we begin to lose. Do you understand?"

Sarah searched her face, then nodded in agreement. She found she not only trusted Laura, but she also admired her as well, and she had a deep-seated sense of obligation for all she was doing for her, Ryan, and her father.

Sarah put her head back, closed her eyes, and willed herself to be calm; it would be over soon enough, and she would be home.

CHAPTER 23

Miriam Bailey sat in the middle of Sarah's bedroom on the floor surrounded by Sarah's things. She had pulled every drawer in the room completely out and flung them carelessly to the floor, emptying them of the contents with blatant disregard. Makeup, clothes, keepsakes, and an array of other items were scattered and piled all over the carpet, but Miriam was looking for very specific things.

She searched and searched until she found what she was looking for: baby powder and candles, both together, under Sarah's bed. The items were exactly what she needed to cast a circle in preparation for the sacrifice of the girl.

Miriam stood and walked back to Kent's room. He sat, bound and gagged, staring at her with a mixture of hatred and concern in his eyes. "Are you feeling a bit, should we say, powerless? Yes? Well, just wait until you see your own flesh and blood being murdered before your very eyes!"

She laughed sadistically and began forming a pentagram with the powder, then encircled it perfectly, chanting incoherently as she went. Next, she took the candles and placed them at each point of the star. She lit each one using a box of matches that had been with them in Sarah's room and continued her chant.

Kent watched in horror as she took her dagger and ran it down the inside of her left arm, the arm that had no wound. Her blood began to flow freely, and she walked around the circle allowing the blood to drip in and around it. When she was finished, a broad, satisfied smile came over her face.

"Priming the pump, so to speak," she said, "Now all I have to do is wait. I think I'll do so downstairs. You may as well relax and let yourself get comfortable; you won't be going anywhere."

Miriam cackled and left the room, leaving Kent to struggle against the ties that held him in place.

∞

With a speeding ticket clutched in her hand, Laura started the car and pulled away from the curb slowly. "Thank God! I thought we would never get out of there!"

Sarah looked at the police car in the side mirror and shook her head. "Well, it's over now, and we can finally go to my dad." She turned to Laura. "I don't know what I would do without you. I don't know how I got myself into this mess; none of this was ever my intention."

"Sarah, the craft is very dangerous, even if you have the best of intentions," Laura told her as she picked up her speed. "Inexperience is one of your greatest enemies, as is lack of knowledge."

Sarah looked out the window and pondered what

Laura had said. If they all got through this without losing their lives, she would make all of this right. She would eliminate the craft from her life, and she would turn back to God. She would beg his forgiveness, and she would allow the hard lessons of life to have their way with her rather than fight them at every turn. She saw now how foolish she had been, resisting the natural course of things.

They pulled into the Hathaway drive minutes later, and both jumped from the car as if it were on fire. They ran to the front door, but it was locked, and Sarah had to dig her keys from her pocket and unlock it. They almost fell into the house when she opened the door.

"Dad!" Sarah yelled as she ran toward the kitchen with Laura at her heels, "Dad!"

With no response, she stopped and turned to Laura. "Maybe he's…"

That was when she saw Miriam. The woman was standing near the foyer with a satisfied look on her face. Laura saw Sarah's eyes grow wide, and she turned around.

"You!" Miriam said as the reality of who she was looking at took hold of her mind. Her smile faded quickly. "I should have known! How many times did my stomach grow nauseous in your presence in the last several years? I couldn't count them if I tried!"

Miriam took a couple of steps toward them, her mind working overtime. "You are the one who has thrown a wrench in my spokes, aren't you? How long have you been a witch, Laura McCain? How long?"

"Not very long," she replied.

Miriam pulled her dagger from behind her back. "Well, I guess this is as good a time as any to put an end to your roving and allow the better woman to step up to the plate. Stay out of my way Laura!"

In a flash, she closed the gap between them and put the knife to Sarah's throat before the girl even knew what was happening. "I have something to show you both. I am sure you will find it very, very interesting. Laura, would you please lead the way upstairs?"

Laura looked at Sarah, whose eyes were filled with fear. "Don't fight her right now, Sarah. Her time will come soon enough." The woman turned and started walking to the staircase, with Miriam and Sarah right behind her.

At the top Miriam said, "Not the first door. We have no need for anything in Sarah's room. Go on to the next."

Laura walked past the door to Sarah's room. As they neared the door to Kent's room, Sarah saw the flickering of candles; her mind knew what she was going to see: this was the place that Miriam intended to offer her to the dark gods. This was the room where the circle had been cast.

They crossed the threshold, and when Kent saw his daughter with a knife to her throat, he began to fight against the ties. The chair he sat in, rocked back and forth on its feet as he struggled.

"No, Dad! You have to relax!" A tear ran down Kent's face as he looked at his daughter. Yes, he was going to witness her death, and then likely experience his own, and there was nothing he could do about it.

"Now Sarah," Miriam began, "go sit in the middle of the circle like a good little girl. This will go much more smoothly for everyone if none of you fight."

She let go of the girl, who turned to look at her with fiery hatred in her eyes. "I hope you burn in hell," Sarah hissed.

Miriam laughed. "Oh, I most certainly will. You can count on that."

Sarah glanced at Laura, who had pretty much faded into the background, all but forgotten by Miriam. Sarah then began to back into the middle of the circle, and she finally sat in the very center of the massive pentagram, giving up her own will. She would rather die than anything else at that point; all of this was because of her, and she knew it. She hated herself at that moment, and death had become a welcome friend in her mind.

Miriam's wicked smile grew as she watched the girl sit. "This could not be more perfect. You have given in so gracefully. If I had a soul to speak of, I would almost feel guilty. But thank the devil I do not."

Miriam closed her eyes and lifted her face to the sky. She began to chant in what seemed to be Latin; Sarah did not understand a word. Her hands were trembling as she watched Miriam go into what appeared to be a trance.

Out of the corner of her eye, she saw Laura moving silently toward Miriam, who appeared blissfully unaware. Sarah's eyes grew even wider as the woman stood up behind the black witch. She reached behind her back, and when her hand came back into sight, it held a dagger, Laura's own dagger. It too was silver, like the one in Miriam's hand, but it was longer and sharper, and it was set with a large black stone in the handle.

Laura reached around the chanting woman, and with one stealth swipe, she laid the black witch's throat wide open.

Miriam's eyes flew open, and a confused look came over her face. Her hand went to her neck, and when she pulled it away, she saw that it was covered in her own blood, which was pumping out like water from a faucet. She looked at Sarah, who was smiling at her.

"Who?" That was the last word Miriam spoke. Her body fell to the floor like a ragdoll, and she died there in a pool of her own blood.

Laura stepped over her body and looked at Sarah, then at Kent. They both returned her gaze; Kent's was one of relief, and Sarah's was one of adoration. Laura smiled.

"So simple," she said, "I have always loved it when all the hard work has been done for me." She looked down at the body of Miriam. "Thank you. You saved me so much time."

She stepped into the circle and knelt before Sarah. "The same old methods of luring become so… tedious and boring century after century. I love to add a little bit of variety." She turned to glance at Miriam briefly. "She was my puppet, and every movement she made was because I tugged her strings."

Laura turned back to Sarah, who was gazing at her with love, then she looked up at Kent, who had a horrified look on his face. "Your daughter is unable to understand, but I know that you do. She has surrendered completely to me, even deep in her soul. If it is any consolation to you, she will not suffer for even a second."

She looked at Sarah. "My dear, though you do not see, all of this was my doing. Miriam was my pawn; she thought she pursued her own ends, but she was never going to succeed. I am the one who lured both you and her. Ryan will live; I want you to know that, though it matters not to you now."

Laura closed her eyes briefly, then looked at Sarah again.

"What once was yours now becomes mine.
The life in your flesh will now be lived by me.
The blood in your veins will soon flow through mine.
It is through your eyes that soon I will see…"

She drew the knife across Sarah's bare neck deftly, and the girl's blood began to flow. She fell over, and it flowed into the circle, which began to glow. Kent screamed through his gag and struggled as his daughter died before his eyes.

Laura was becoming younger. The lines in her face smoothed out, and her hair darkened rapidly. The soft rolls of her forty-seven-year-old body disappeared like magic, and her clothing soon hung off her like rags. She stood and stretched, strength and pleasure coursing through her veins.

"So willing she was," Laura said to Kent, "She was an angel, She died with love in her heart for me. Pity I had none to return. I am pleased with her taste in clothing; I will have to borrow something." She grimaced as she caught her own reflection in the mirror.

"I would apologize for all of this, but the truth is, I feel no sorrow or remorse." She walked to the struggling man and quickly buried her dagger in his chest. "But it's the least I can do to put you out of your misery. You've given so much to my cause."

Laura McCain left the room nearly floating in ecstasy. She took a filmy black dress from Sarah's closet and quickly changed into it. She could feel grief and sorrow exuding from it, and she knew it had been worn to the girl's mother's funeral.

"How appropriate," she said to her reflection smugly.

With that, Laura McCain left the house. She climbed into her car and drove away, humming with satisfaction.

CHAPTER 24

The rain fell in drizzles from a slate-gray sky in Paradise, Ohio.

It was a large funeral, and it seemed that the entire small town was in attendance. There was not a dry eye as the pastor of Our Heaven's Gospel Church from the nearby town of Aticka conducted the service. After all, this family had known nothing but misfortune and suffering the last few years of their lives.

Kate Morris stood with her husband and son. Her hand was on Ryan's shoulder; he was sobbing and shaking violently. He would get past this; after all, he was so young. Kate was so grateful that it wasn't he who was being eulogized that day. That was all she cared about.

But Ryan wanted Sarah back. His heart was broken, and if there was a God, he hated Him. Ryan had not been raised in the church, and he had no memory or understanding of the things that had taken place in Paradise while he was in the hospital. It only made sense to him to continue in the craft Sarah had brought into his life. That was how he would keep her alive.

The attendees of the funeral began to disperse, all of

them making their way back to their vehicles in the cold winter rain.

Paradise would live to see another day…

∞

"Know that God loves you, and He has a very special plan for the lives of each and every one of you. Go forth this week in the blessings of God." Pastor Gary Kemp of the Assembly of the Lord church in Heavenly, Wyoming smiled at his congregation. "Before we leave, I would like to give a great big Assembly welcome to our new church secretary. Laura McCain, we are glad to make you a part of the family!"

The church broke into applause, and everyone in the congregation turned and smiled in the direction of the slight red-haired young woman at the end of the front row. She nodded and smiled shyly, even blushing a bit in humility.

"Thank you for having me," she said as the applause died, "I can only hope to serve all of you as you deserve."

She sat back down and turned her eyes to the pastor as he proceeded to say the closing prayer. As the rest of the congregation bowed their heads, Laura McCain stared straight ahead, and she smiled…

Lucifer's Angel

ENTREATY

This book was made possible by reviews from readers like you. Reviews fuel my creativity. If you enjoyed this novel, I implore you to please write a review and share your experience on the retailer's website. The livelihood for authors is entirely dependent on reviews, and I must say, it is the largest obstacle as a struggling author that I have encountered. Please tell a friend, tell a loved one about this read. With your help, I will be one step closer to overcoming this obstacle. In return, I thank you from the bottom of my heart, and sincerely appreciate your time and effort.

Humbled, with gratitude,

R.W.K. Clark

ABOUT THE AUTHOR

I am a father of two beautiful children, Jon and Kim. They are my motivating forces; they are the lighthouse in this vast ocean. In my life, they are the air that I breathe; they are the oasis in this desert of uncertainty. They are my greatest joy in life and my number one priority. I have a long list of hobbies, and I attribute that to my lust for life! I like to surround myself with positive people, who share the same interests. Family values, the arts, outdoors, nature, and travel are tops on my list. I embrace attending cultural and artistic events because I believe dramatic self-expression is the window to the soul. I wear my heart on my sleeve, and I still believe in chivalry, and I always treat people the way I want to be treated.

www.rwkclark.com